"Then a you did with him any different than what you did with me?"

"I really don't know, Drew." She was tempted to tell him to go to hell, but her honesty won out. "But I can tell you what they had in common. Both times I was thinking about you."

She'd had enough of this conversation. She rose from the sofa, intending to go to the bedroom. Let him sleep out here if that was what he wanted. Damn him.

She made it as far as the hallway before he caught up with her, grasping her forearm to bring her around to face him. "What do you mean, you were thinking about me?"

Did she have to spell it out for him? That something about this case, about him, had been getting to her? Too bad. She couldn't think of a coherent way to explain it. All she could manage was a baleful, "Drew…"

For a moment he didn't say anything, but the heat in his gaze was enough. He wanted her, and God help her, she wanted him, too.

Books by Deirdre Savoy

Kimani Romance

An Innocent Man
Forbidden Games

DEIRDRE SAVOY

is a native New Yorker who spent her summers on the shores of Martha's Vineyard, soaking up the sun and scribbling in one of her many notebooks. It was there that she first started writing romance stories as a teenager. Since then, Deirdre has published ten books, all of which have garnered critical acclaim and honors. She lives in Bronx, New York, with her husband and their two children. In her spare time she enjoys reading, dancing, calligraphy and "wicked" crossword puzzles.

forbidden games

deirdre savoy

To the world's best fans, my readers. Thank you.
And for Ralph Smith, a good guy from
the neighborhood who stayed good.

 KIMANI PRESS™

ISBN-13: 978-0-373-86101-9
ISBN-10:   0-373-86101-X

Recycling programs
for this product may
not exist in your area.

FORBIDDEN GAMES

Copyright © 2009 by Deirdre Savoy

www.kimanipress.com

Printed in U.S.A.

Dear Reader,

I hope you enjoy reading Zaria and Drew's story as much as I enjoyed writing it.

I always love to hear from readers. Please contact me at deesavoy@gmail.com or at:

P.O. Box 233

Bronx, NY 10469

Wishing you all love, romance and a little suspense.

All the best,

Deirdre Savoy

Prologue

She would only have this one chance.

She knew that as sure as she'd spent the last few months ingratiating herself with them, offering them no trouble, making them trust her. And now her time had come. They'd taken her out of one of the back rooms and let her work in the front, greeting the customers. That in itself had been a great plus, but she wanted out. She wanted freedom.

Now there was a problem with one of the girls and they'd forgotten about her. Whatever it was, it happened so fast and in the wrong language and she couldn't make out what was going on.

It didn't really matter, though. The guard that usually sat by the door had been called to the back. It would be an easy thing to do, to simply open the front door and slip out. This wasn't the way she'd planned things, but it would have to do.

Later the surveillance tape would tell the truth, but for now she was unconcerned. She took the money from the cash box under the counter and slipped it into her panties. It wasn't much, but it beat nothing at all. Quietly, she rounded the counter, her eyes on the hallway leading to the back. No one was coming. No one was even looking in her direction. She crossed herself for protection as anticipation filled her.

She was out the door in the next second, breathing in the cool midnight air as she hurried down the block. Each morning when the bus dropped them off, she'd studied the area, trying to plan an escape route. But it was dark now and her bearings were off. She still thought she knew how to make it to the taxi stand she passed every day. She had no idea if taxis still ran this late, but she had to chance it.

But where would she go? She had no family here, no friends, nowhere to stay. She couldn't go to the police for help. Then she'd end up where she started. She'd die before she let them send her back. She'd head into the city. The money she'd stolen would surely pay for one night in a hotel while she figured out what to do.

With a plan formed in her mind, she focused on her surroundings, noticing for the first time the car pulling up behind her. It was black, familiar and bore a license plate she recognized. *¡Madre de Dios!* Her departure hadn't gone unnoticed. They'd come after her.

The car screeched to a halt beside her, but she was already running. They were in a commercial district that boasted long alleyways and dark passages and she hoped to get lost in one of them. As soon as she was able, she darted right into one alley, hoping she hadn't chosen a dead end. She could hear them behind her, calling after her, the heavy tread of their shoes slapping against the pavement. All she had on her feet were a pair of flip-flops that pinched her feet and slowed her down, but she couldn't stop, couldn't let them catch her. She knew what would await her.

She darted to the left, down another corridor, but she could feel them behind her. Her lungs felt ready to explode and her legs were tiring. She pressed on, around another corner, then… *THWACK!*

The sudden blow to her face snapped her head back, stunning her. Dizzily, as if in slow motion, she spun around, lost her footing and came down hard on her knees. Her face was damp from the tears that sprang to her eyes and the blood and mucus that flowed from her broken nose. Automatically, her hand rose to wipe it away, but she only managed to blur her own vision.

It hadn't occurred to her that the men had split up, but that was the only explanation for her easy capture. The man she'd heard behind her joined them, his breathing heavy. He yanked her hair, twisting her face up so that she could see his. *"¿Adónde piensas ir?"*

Where did she think she was going? Before she had time to give the answer any consideration, he hauled her to her feet. But she couldn't let it end like this. She'd come too close. With her nails and fists she fought him until he released her hair. The other man tried to grab her, but a knee to his groin felled him. Then she was running again, back the way she'd come, anywhere. She only knew she couldn't let them take her back.

And they wouldn't. She heard the sound of the gunshot at the same time the bullet pierced her body. She stumbled forward, falling clumsily into a puddle with a dull splash. Her hands had done nothing to break her fall. Her face lay in that dirty water, but she didn't care. She didn't care as she heard the men approach her and one of them used his foot to roll her over. She smiled up at them. It wouldn't be long now. She knew that as sure as she knew her life's blood was now seeping out of her body. She had gotten her wish. One way or another, she would be free.

Chapter 1

"You ready to roll?"

Andrew Grissom slowly lowered the copy of the *Times* he'd been reading and turned his head in the direction of the husky female voice. The first thing he noticed were the long, long legs encased in black fishnet stockings. Above that, black spandex shorts clung to shapely hips beneath a fitted top that barely contained Zaria Fuentes's ample cleavage and exposed a good three inches of her midriff. Frizzy jet-black hair floated around her shoulders. Aside from looking sexy as hell, it served as a hiding place for a mike.

He focused on her face: exotic, almond-shaped amber eyes underneath winged brows, cheekbones for days and a pair of lips that would send Pam Anderson running back for collagen injections—all coated in more makeup than she usually wore in a week.

Drew swallowed. He was ready, all right. Even without the war paint and the Hookers R Us get-up, Zaria was a knockout. That fact wasn't lost on any member of the team, but acknowledging that in any serious way was likely to get him a sock in the gut.

"For you, baby, anytime," he drawled.

Zaria rolled her eyes, but it was just for show. He knew she didn't take him seriously, which allowed him the freedom to say whatever nonsense popped into his head. "Keep dreaming, Grissom. Maybe then it will happen."

"Promises, promises." He pushed to his feet off the crappy sofa in the corner of the 41st precinct's basement and tossed the paper onto one of the cushions. In the three-inch heels she wore, Zaria topped six feet, but still only reached his shoulder. "Where's Schraft?" he asked, referring to the sergeant who led their team.

"Everybody's out by the van waiting for you, Lazybones."

That figured. Everyone was anxious to get on with the day's work. They'd gotten a tip on one Levar Alston getting his mama to sell crack and weed out of an apartment on East 173rd while he had his sister and a couple of cousins out selling something else. Apparently, Levar liked to keep it in the family, which might have been a mistake, considering that when the sister got picked up a few days ago she rolled on everybody else.

Now he, Zaria and the rest of their team were headed out to pay Mr. Alston a little visit. Unlike Narcotics, who tended to focus on the bigger fish and the bigger money, building cases over weeks or months, their squad focused on getting the dealers and their customers off the streets with surveillance, buy-and-busts and the like. You didn't have to work up elaborate cases against someone who made the mistake of selling you a couple of hundred dollars' worth of crack. You could just haul them in and hope to make a charge stick. Considering the sister had already rolled, that wouldn't be too much of a problem.

Zaria had volunteered to do the buy, figuring Alston might offer her a spot in his depleted stable and then they'd have their hooks into him for that, too. Drew agreed with her that he might. Half the hookers he knew got into the business as a means to satisfy a habit. The other half were introduced to it by their pimps to keep them in line. But he knew that wasn't what really interested Zaria. Her ambition led her to look for opportunities to shine for the higher-ups—anything that might lead to that detective's shield she craved. Sometimes he wondered if that didn't make her take chances she shouldn't.

It didn't take them long to set up. O'Malley and the sarge were with the van around the corner. Bruno was in a parked car at the end of the block. He and Frisk were on a rooftop providing surveillance and cover, if necessary.

Drew shifted his weight for a better vantage point and looked through his binoculars. He had a clear view of the front of the apartment building, including the entranceway where a kid stood with his hands in the pockets of low-slung jeans. He was the gatekeeper, the one to tell you which of three apartments Alston was selling out of that day. Even if you could make it into the building without direction, showing up at the wrong door on the wrong day couldn't be a good thing.

Their positions had been decided yesterday, before this feeling of apprehension had gripped him. He hadn't been happy about it then. No one wanted to play lookout, or worse, sit in the hot van while they waited for it to fill with whatever skels and other scumbags they picked up coming out of the apartment after a sale. For about a minute he'd thought to ask to swap spots with Bruno or even one of the guys in the van—anything to be down on the ground and closer to the action. But none of the guys would have done that without an explanation. Since he wasn't prepared to give one, he hadn't bothered. But it didn't make him feel any better.

"Do you see her?" Frisk asked with a bit more avidness in his voice than Drew cared for.

Drew glanced over his shoulder at the kid and scowled. Zaria wanted her shield. Bruno had joined the squad looking for a less demanding tour than Narcotics. The sarge was just waiting to count down his twenty before retiring. Frisk apparently couldn't see beyond the possibility of watching a hot piece of ass. Drew ground his teeth together. Was he the only one focused on doing the actual job?

He almost voiced his sentiments out loud, but considering no one, not even Frisk, would buy that sentiment coming from him, he didn't bother. He knew the rest of them considered him a bit of a rogue, not knowing the meaning of the word *teamwork*, despite working with a team. Zaria in particular viewed him as being too laid-back, too quick with a flip comment, unwilling to work himself up too much over anything he didn't find worthwhile. To some extent they were right. He wasn't about to put his ass on the line for anyone who didn't deserve it, nor was he willing to kiss anyone else's to get ahead.

Anyone paying more attention to his record than to his mouth would know how wrong that assessment was. He'd been offered choicer gigs and turned them down. What he did was worthwhile and he was good at it. What the hell else did a guy need?

He nodded toward the camera around the kid's neck, which was used to document who came and went when it came time to go to court. You couldn't very well claim you hadn't been at an apartment buying smack while an eight-by-ten glossy said otherwise.

He said to Frisk, "Are you going to talk, or are you going to use that thing?"

Drew looked through his binoculars in time to see a tall, skinny man in dirty jeans and a black T-shirt coming out of the building. He slapped hands with the kid outside before heading up the block toward them. "You got him?" Drew asked, and was rewarded by the sound of a few shots being clicked off on the 35 mm camera.

Drew keyed his mike to speak to the other members of the team. "Homey in a black bag headed your way."

"Roger," came the response, probably from the sarge, but with that one word it was hard to tell. Either way, with any luck they'd grab up this guy for processing later.

Drew checked his watch. It shouldn't be long before Zaria went in. Not to disappoint, Schraft's voice came over the headset. "It's a go."

Instantly, Drew's body tensed. It would probably amount to nothing, this feeling in his gut, but he'd been right often enough to trust whatever reaction came first. At least it would be over soon. He saw her then, striding down the block, but without her usual long-legged, confident stride. Her walk was more rapid, less sure, as if she were agitated or strung out. It was all part of the show, intended to fool the kid at the door, as was the lollipop tucked in the corner of her mouth—a distraction.

"Damn. I never wanted to be a lollipop so bad before," Frisk said.

Drew slid him a quelling glance. At least the kid had his gaze focused through the viewfinder this time. Still, he could live without another man voicing the thoughts in his own mind. Not that Zaria would ever have given either of them the time of day. She treated Frisk like a stray puppy; she treated him like some incorrigible younger brother who'd grown too big to discipline.

Now he had more important matters to focus on besides Zaria's assets threatening to pop out of her top. Though they stepped into danger every day, what Zaria was about to do could be dangerous. There were lots of ways a cop could burn their cover, the least of which was being recognized by some perp they were trying to bring down.

She pulled the lollipop from her mouth. "Hey, baby, what's cracking?" she said.

The kid licked his lips, his eyes avid. "Depends. Whatchu want?"

Drew didn't bother to focus on the words that came next. The kid was going to let her up, if only to have an excuse to watch her come back down. She stepped inside the building, but it was a few seconds before they heard anything else from her.

"I'm in," she said in a hushed tone.

A statement of the obvious, but at least that let them know she was alone, probably in the elevator. Even before her meet and greet with the kid downstairs they'd known which apartment Alston was dealing from, courtesy of one of the skels they'd picked up earlier. She was headed to the fourth floor, the last apartment on the far side of the building—probably the worst location, considering where they'd set up, but it couldn't be helped now.

The next sound he heard was a slow grinding noise, probably the elevator door opening. Apparently someone was waiting to take the ride down, since the sound of voices reached him. "This is it."

Zaria's voice sounded too confident to please him. Too much could go wrong and she had that reckless thing going on, besides. But soon enough, she was inside the apartment. Her job was to score a few rocks and then get the hell out, though he knew she'd give Alston the chance to come on to her. She'd succeeded in the first part of the job when he noticed a man on the street talking to the lookout.

Damn. He'd prefer it if Zaria got out before anyone else went in. More bodies in the apartment meant more things could go wrong. But she was taking her time, letting Alston lay his rap on her about working off her habit in trade. So far, nothing he'd said would mean a damn thing in a court of law, nor probably would he. She needed to get out of there. He would have told her that if he had any means of doing so. But she was only set to transmit, not receive.

The guy on the street disappeared into the building just as it appeared Zaria was giving up the ghost. Thank God for small favors. But she didn't make it out before the new mark hit the door. From listening to Zaria's wire, they'd ascertained there were three men in the room—Alston and two others who undoubtedly served as muscle if any trouble broke out. Mama must have had the day off. One of them, not Alston, shouted, "Hey, I know this son of a bitch. He's five-oh."

For an instant Drew froze. Damn. The new guy had been made as a cop. Just what they needed. A second later, the sound of gunfire, shouting and chaos crackled in the headset.

"Everybody, go," the sarge said in a clear but urgent voice. "Go now."

Drew was already on his feet, all six foot seven, two hundred sixty pounds of him running toward the side of the building where a ladder led down to the fire escape. He made it down, taking two steps at a time. He hit the ground, still running, heading toward the curb. Simultaneously, he drew his gun and flashed his badge at oncoming motorists as he crossed into the street. He was big enough that no one could miss him, but he wasn't taking any chances. At least that's what he thought. The next thing he knew, he was airborne—not quite an unpleasant experience. It was the last thing he remembered for a long, long time.

Chapter 2

Even before Drew opened his eyes he knew where he was. The particular brand of antiseptic smell only came with doing time in a hospital. He also knew he wasn't alone. The scent of a familiar perfume reached his nostrils. He popped one eye open. "Hey," he said.

The delicate woman standing beside his bed punched him in the arm. "Hey, yourself. What the hell is wrong with you?"

He'd have asked her if she wanted the short list or the long one, except his cousin-in-law, Carly, didn't look in the mood for jokes. "Why don't you ask the Mack truck that hit me?"

"Not funny," she said, but her expression softened. "How are you feeling?"

He shifted to assess the damage. Only his left hip and the right side of his head hurt. "I've been worse."

"Thank goodness for that."

"Where's Jackson?" he asked, referring to his cousin, her husband.

"Outside talking with your crew. They're all here, I think."

That was to be expected, but he'd deal with them later. "Let me talk to Jackson for a minute, okay?"

She frowned. "I'm not through with you yet, though."

He didn't doubt that. Carly had managed to lasso Jackson and civilize him and was determined to do the same with him. He didn't imagine she appreciated him allowing himself to get hurt on the job, even if a vehicle, not a villain, was responsible.

Carly left and a moment later Jackson came in. Jackson was nearly as tall as Drew, but with a different, more wiry build. When they were kids, Drew had used the threat of his greater size to keep his younger cousin in line, but it had been a long time since that tactic worked. Drew wished he still had that advantage as Jackson pulled a chair over to his bedside, since there was more amusement than concern in his expression.

Jackson sat back, steepling his fingers. "I thought we had a pact, buddy."

What seemed like a lifetime ago, he and Jackson had vowed to be more careful since they were the only family either of them had anymore. But that was no longer true for Jackson. He had Carly and a beautiful little girl they all adored. But Drew didn't want any of them worrying about him, especially since as far as he knew all he'd sustained was a bruised hip and a slight concussion when his head hit the pavement. He hadn't lied to Carly—he'd been banged up much worse.

Drew said, "Wasn't my idea. How'd the driver make out?"

"I don't think she'll be putting makeup on while she's driving anymore. At least not for a while. You damn near totaled her car."

Drew chuckled. "What can I tell you? Must be all those vitamins Mama kept feeding me."

"Yeah, well, I heard they're keeping you overnight. Carly and I want you to stay with us until you're back on your feet."

Drew cast his cousin a skeptical look. More than likely Jackson had already cornered the doctor and made him confess all he knew. And as for the invite, it was a flimsy excuse for Carly to get her busy eyes on him and probably foist some more eligible women on him in which he had no interest. No thanks. Besides, he intended to get back on the job as soon as possible. "I'll be fine."

Jackson stood. "Suit yourself. Carly's going to be disappointed."

He'd bet, but he knew Jackson was trying to guilt him. "She'll get over it."

Jackson shrugged. "I'm sure she will." He extended a hand toward Drew, which he shook. "Call me if you need anything."

"Will do."

"Some other folks are waiting to see you."

As Jackson departed the others came in. The sarge claimed the one chair in the room. Bruno and O'Malley stood at the foot of his bed. Frisk was fiddling with the blinds. The only person who wasn't in the room was the one person he wanted to see. He thought of asking about her, but didn't want to invite speculation.

"How are you doing?" Schraft asked.

He gave his usual response. "I've been worse." What came next didn't surprise him—a first-class ribbing about not only getting hit but nearly wrecking the car that mowed him down. He supposed he deserved it, considering that if he'd been paying more attention to his own safety as opposed to Zaria's, he could have avoided getting hit in the first place.

Still, his concern wasn't for himself. If things had really gone south in that apartment, he was sure he'd have heard about it already, but he wanted to know. "How'd the bust go down?"

The sarge frowned. "Turns out somebody messed up and gave the case to both us and the narcs. They made a move at about the same time we did. After the other cop was made, all hell broke loose."

"Zaria made it out okay?"

"Man, she not only made it out," Frisk said with a note of awe and respect in his voice. "She not only took down two of the assholes in the room, she saved the other cop's behind, too."

That sounded like her—Superwoman in hot pants. He admitted it to himself, feeling the same admiration he heard in Frisk's voice. "Who got the collar?"

"Narcs," a couple of the guys said in unison.

Mentally, Drew shrugged. That seemed about right. Not only was the narc squad a bit higher on the police food chain than their ragtag squad was, it seemed fitting that the team that did the least work garnered the most credit. "Where is she?"

"Zaria? By now she's probably home."

Drew shrugged, not wanting to let the disappointment he felt show.

"We'd better be going, too." The sarge stood, glancing at the others in a way that suggested it was time to go.

Drew shook their hands and endured the few parting shots the guys offered. When they were gone, he leaned back on his pillows, feeling restless. He felt achy but well enough to go home. He had a vague memory of being asked if he lived alone. Answering "yes" probably hadn't been a wise thing, since they'd decided to keep him. He probably should have let Jackson and Carly spring him, but he didn't want to put them out, either. If only someone would show up and hook up a damn TV, he could at least entertain himself with some mindless fluff.

Or maybe not. His mind was still focused on Zaria—the chances she'd taken that morning, her bravery in saving another cop's life, but mostly the fact that she hadn't bothered to come see him and whatever the reason for that was. He wanted to see her to make sure for himself that she was all right. He would have felt that way about any member of their team under similar circumstances, which was why the others had shown up to see him. You put your face in the door and checked on each other, if only for a few minutes.

But she hadn't come. He hoped it wasn't because the day had been too much for her.

Drew shifted, then groaned from the stiffness in his leg. Yeah, he could see Zaria, the Iron Maiden, falling apart. Not in this lifetime. If anything, she was probably annoyed at him for getting hurt and diverting attention from her bust. Then to have the narcs steal it must have really burned her butt. She was probably too ticked to bother with him.

And he had to admit the exercise of professional courtesy wasn't the only reason he wished she'd shown up. They'd worked together for the past two years and joked around a lot. They'd become close in a way that other members of the team were not. He'd met her grandmother and she'd met Carly and Jackson. They were friends of a sort.

But in the last couple of months, his feelings for her had shifted. He'd started noticing her as a woman, not only as a cop. That wasn't exactly true, either. He'd always been aware of her as a woman. He would have to be half-blind or dead not to notice her. What he'd never considered was her as *his* woman.

He knew exactly when it started. She'd broken up with one

of those buttoned-down types she loved to date. She'd called it off, but he could see that she was bothered by it. Drew had wanted to hunt the guy down and let him have it. Not that Zaria would have appreciated that or couldn't have done it herself if that's what she'd wanted. That's when this proprietary urge toward her had started.

Luckily for him, she didn't seem to notice. She regarded him as she always had—a big nuisance, but one of which she was fond. That used to be enough for him, but things had changed for him. He hadn't done anything about it since he wasn't her type, she'd already started seeing someone else and besides, he didn't want to ruin the good thing they had going. Maybe it was for the best that she hadn't bothered to come. What he needed most of all was to get his head right where she was concerned before he did something stupid.

There was a knock at the door and a second later Zaria poked her head in.

"Hey," he said.

"Hey, yourself," she said, coming fully into the room. She wore a pair of jeans and a T-shirt with her jacket slung over one arm. As she walked toward him, she dropped the jacket in the chair. "What was that this afternoon, anyway?"

She stood by his bedside with her hands on her hips and a no-nonsense expression on her face. Was every woman he saw today going to bear the same expression?

Just to annoy her, he said, "To what are you referring?"

"What, did you develop a sudden death wish this afternoon? Frisk said he didn't know you could move that fast."

"Was that before or after I went airborne? And here I thought someone would appreciate my coming to the aid of a fellow officer in trouble."

Zaria rolled her eyes. "I can take care of myself."

"Obviously." Was that the only reason she'd come—to scold him for what she saw as his own foolhardiness? "So what's up with you? Did you see the shrink yet?" he asked, knowing it was part of the drill after a shooting.

She pushed her jacket aside and sat, propping her feet on the underside of the bed. "That's where I'm coming from. I wanted to get it over with." She rubbed her eyes with her fingertips. "You don't look too much the worse for wear." She grinned. "Although I heard about you wrecking that poor woman's car."

"I'm never going to live that down, am I?"

"Not in this lifetime." She dropped her feet to the floor and sat forward. "Seriously, I appreciate the effort, but I think I speak for the team when I say we'd rather have you in one piece." She stood. "When are you going to be back?"

"Dunno. I get sprung from here tomorrow, but I'll probably take a couple days off." She cast him a scoffing look. The only time he'd ever taken off was to help out his cousin Jackson a few years back when he and Carly had gotten into some trouble. "Why?" he asked.

"I want to know how soon to replace the stash from your candy-bar drawer."

Despite the flippancy of her tone he realized she'd worried about him, if only a little. "Forget about it. I'm thinking of switching to chips, anyway."

She shrugged. "See you, then."

She picked up her jacket and left. Drew stared after her. That had to be the most stilted conversation the two of them had ever had. And if he wasn't mistaken, there was more on her mind than recklessness on either of their parts. That's what bothered him now. Something else weighed on her that she refused to share with him. He speculated about what that might be until a member of the hospital staff, a petite woman in a white shirt and khaki pants, came into the room.

"Ready to have your TV set up?" she asked.

"For you, baby, anytime," he drawled, but he only reminded himself of Zaria.

Chapter 3

Zaria let herself into her apartment and dropped her keys onto the small console table beside the door. She kicked the door closed as she continued to scan the mail she'd picked up downstairs. Nothing but bills and advertisements. She dropped the mail onto the table, as well, and looked down. Her cat, Scratchy, was winding itself around her legs, showing his appreciation of her being home.

She stooped and picked up the cat, which was barely older than a kitten. She'd found him meowing on her fire escape one day and made the mistake of feeding him. He returned each day, scratching at her window with such persistence that she let him in. He'd been her adoring companion ever since.

She brought the cat up to eye level. "What have you been up to, young man?" The cat meowed and licked its lips. The poor thing was probably starving since she hadn't been home since that morning and it was past his dinnertime now. She went to the kitchen to pour some food into his dish and refresh the water. Scratchy forgot all about her while he settled down to dine.

It was just as well, since she wasn't in the mood for company, either feline or human. It had been a long, harrowing day by any standard. She'd awoken that morning to find herself alone for the first time in a few weeks, having endured her first and last fight with James Dalton Harrison, the lawyer she'd been dating, the night before. Truthfully, she couldn't remember now what had set them off. She only remembered sitting across from him at her dinner table and feeling irritated. He was everything she told herself she wanted: ambitious, financially stable and from a good family. All those things her own parents could have used a good dose of.

Both her parents had abandoned her in one way or another. Her father had simply disappeared; her mother had drowned in a bottle. Zaria had mostly fended for herself, with a little help from her grandmothers. So now when she looked at a man, she mostly saw his prospects, what he could do for her and whatever children she might have. Or that had been the case until last night when she'd thrown Harrison out. She'd known she didn't really care for him and never would despite his meeting her demographic profile of the ideal man.

So, aside from Scratchy, she was alone again, and maybe it was best if it stayed that way for a while. No buppie like Harrison could grasp what she did for a living every day. He'd as much as said that what she did was a waste of time considering the ease with which he and his ilk could get the average drug dealer off.

The only person in whom she considered confiding had been Drew. He was the only person she could tell how scared she'd been without having him think less of her. Even the rest of the guys on the team looked at her differently because she was a woman. Half of them wanted to bed her and the other half viewed any fear or emotion on her part as a sign of feminine weakness. Only Drew viewed her as an equal.

Or he had. Lately she didn't know what was up with him, either. She only knew he wouldn't have risked life and limb the same way running in after one of the guys. Something between them had changed. Until she figured out what it was, she'd keep her distance from him, too.

When she got up to get ready for bed, Scratchy followed to claim a spot on the pillow next to hers. Zaria laughed and petted the cat. He wasn't the man of her dreams, but for tonight he would have to do.

The next morning Zaria descended the stairs to their base-ment office a half hour early, carrying a box of joe and an assorted dozen doughnuts. Most of the guys couldn't make a cup of coffee worth a damn and she didn't feel like bothering herself. She set her goodies down in the break room, which was mostly a long counter in an alcove that afforded no privacy.

After she'd poured herself a cup and snagged a strawberry frosted doughnut, she headed to her desk. From that vantage point she saw Sergeant Schraft talking with two men in dark suits, Feebs probably from the look of them. They definitely weren't NYPD unless they were way up on the food chain. Regular cops didn't rock Armani.

Whatever was going on, she could live with it as long as it didn't involve her. She'd had enough excitement the day before. She didn't even have her gun back yet. Pulling out her copy of the *Times,* she leaned back in her chair. Let it be someone else's turn for a change.

Luck wasn't with her, however. A few moments later, the sarge poked his head out the office door. "Officer Fuentes, can I speak with you for a moment, please?"

"Sure." She put down the paper and walked toward the office. As she approached, she surveyed the two men more closely. Both had olive complexions, though one appeared to be His-panic, the other Italian, maybe. She couldn't tell by their demeanor which man was of higher rank, but the Hispanic man approached her first.

"Officer Fuentes," he said, extending his hand toward her. "I'm Agent Gonzales from Immigration and this is Agent Spenser of the FBI."

Zaria shook each man's hand. So she was off with the Italian. Her gaze slid to Schraft. He nodded, indicating she should go along. "What can I do for you boys?"

They moved aside to allow her to sit in one of the visitor chairs. Gonzales sat beside her while Spenser stood beside Schraft's desk, facing her.

Gonzales leaned closer to her. "Three days ago firefighters were called to the site of a supposed beauty spa on Haven Road in the Sunnyside section of Queens. When the smoke cleared, the bodies of three women were found. We haven't been able to identify two of the women. One was shot in the chest. The other had her throat slit. The third woman was Rosa Perez." Gonzales pulled a picture from a folder she hadn't realized he carried. He laid the photograph on Schraft's desk in front of her.

Zaria picked up the picture. Perez appeared to be in her early forties, with long, dark, wavy hair and enough eyeliner to do Cleopatra proud. There was also something hard in her pretty face.

Zaria tossed the picture on the desk. Remembering what Gonzales said about the "supposed spa," Zaria asked, "Who was she? The madam?" These days, old-style massage parlors had given way to nail salons, spas and other types of businesses as a way to camouflage their real activity—prostitution. One way to tell the difference between the legit and the non was to observe the clientele. If you got mostly men tromping through a nail salon, you could bet your last money they weren't there for the mani-pedi special.

"Something like that," Gonzales said. "She ran the day-to-day operations, but we know she wasn't the owner. We credit that to a man named Jaime Acevedo." Gonzales produced another photograph. This picture featured a medium close-up of a man dressed in a dark business suit beneath a camel-colored coat. It was in black and white and the subject didn't appear to be aware his picture was being taken. If she weren't mistaken, it was probably a surveillance photo courtesy of one of the two men's agencies.

But there was also no mistaking that she knew this man. A lifetime ago she'd known him as Jimmy Vega. He'd lived two floors up from her on Marion Avenue until his family had moved away when his mother remarried. She tossed this photo on top of the other. "What's little Jimmy got to do with this?"

For the first time Spenser spoke. "Little Jimmy, as you call him, is involved in a lot of businesses, most of them cash-based. We have reason to believe that along with prostitution he's laundering drug money for some of the big boys."

Zaria sat back in her chair and whistled. "Who'd have thunk it? Jimmy's most prodigious talents were picking his nose and making fart noises with his armpit."

Schraft cleared his throat. "He seems to have advanced his talents since then."

Apparently. But that wasn't what concerned her at the moment. "What makes you think Jimmy is involved?"

"Chatter coming from the place."

That came from Gonzales again. So they'd had him under surveillance as she'd already supposed, but hadn't produced anything they could make stick. She asked a variant of the first question she'd asked. "What does this have to do with me?"

Gonzales was back to doing the talking. "We want you to infiltrate his operation, find out what he's up to. We figure you'll have a better shot at it due to your acquaintance."

No kidding. That's what she'd thought they were leading up to. She'd done enough undercover work to merit the offer, plus she knew the target. It would make sense, if it weren't so easy for him to find out she was a cop. He knew her by her real name. No chance for fudging. "All he'd have to do is search Google for my name to find out I'm a cop."

"Didn't he know you as Zaria Bennett, before you took back your mother's maiden name?"

That came from Spenser. With his basso profundo voice she didn't have to guess why he kept his mouth shut most of the time. But it appeared the Feebs didn't know everything. She'd taken her grandmother's maiden name as a teenager as a way of rejecting either of her parents' claim to her. But that did change things in a way she didn't appreciate. "I can see how the FBI figures in this, but Immigration?" She fastened a look on Gonzales.

"It seems Acevedo may also be involved in smuggling immigrants across the border for the purpose of entering them into prostitution."

Zaria shook her head. She'd heard of that happening—women forced to pay their passage to America on their backs in deplorable conditions or kidnapped and sold to whoever would pay. "I thought that only happened to Asian women."

Gonzales looked grim. "Depends on where in the city you go. In Chinatown or Little Korea you get Asians, in other neighborhoods you get Russians. In other communities you get Mexicans. There's no shortage of men willing to take advantage of vulnerable women."

Zaria couldn't argue there. And if they'd been trying to prey on her one vulnerability where police work was concerned they'd hit the mark. She thought of her grandmother, who'd emigrated to New York as a young woman from Puerto Rico. Her family had come from money so she hadn't been an easy target for men like those Gonzales described. Her mistake had been marrying a man who ran through everything she had before departing—and raising a daughter who made the same mistake. If Zaria had a chance to bring down these men she knew she would take it.

A slight smile tilted her lips as she said, "Tell me exactly what you want me to do."

Chapter 4

Drew eased into his chair with a groan of relief. Despite having released himself from his hospital stay without benefit of medical expertise, his leg ached, today more from the knee than the hip. Whatever. They were taking their sweet time getting to him and he didn't feel like sticking around. He'd gone home for a change of clothes then hopped in a cab to the precinct. His only concession to his injuries was to walk with a cane he'd acquired the last time he'd gotten himself banged up.

"There he is," Bruno said. "Hope you didn't take down any SUVs on the way in."

"Nah, it's too early in the day for that," Frisk countered, pretending to scan his watch. "Give him another couple hours."

"Real funny, folks," Drew drawled. He nodded in the direction of Schraft's office, where Zaria was in a conference with Schraft and two other men. "How long has that been going on?"

Frisk shrugged. "Since before we got here."

Since both men usually came in around eight and it was now almost nine, that could have been some time. Whatever was going on in there, he was sure he didn't like it. He only hoped the brass weren't questioning her shoot. That could lead to a heck of a lot of trouble, but he didn't think that was the case. The two suits inside didn't strike him as IAB or brass. They damn sure weren't the Publisher's Clearing House Prize Patrol, either.

But the confab or whatever it was appeared to be breaking up. The two suits stood to shake hands with Schraft first and then Zaria. They filed out of the office and up the stairs, casting disparaging looks throughout the office as they went.

Ignoring them, Drew turned his attention back to Zaria. He noticed Schraft slide her gun to her across the desk. She stood and holstered it, nodding at something he said. A moment later she came out of the office. His eyes followed Zaria as she slid into the seat across from him.

"What are you doing here?" she asked him. "Shouldn't you still be in the hospital?"

He shrugged. "What did your new friends want?"

She took a sip from her cup and made a face. "A little UC work, if you must know."

Drew shrugged again. That possibility hadn't occurred to him and he didn't like it too much now that it did. "Doing what?"

"Bringing down some dirtbag luring young women across the border into a life of prostitution."

He knew Zaria. If they'd asked, she'd said yes, and her answer wouldn't have had anything to do with her ambitions. Nothing got Zaria going like the mistreatment of her fellow females. She wouldn't even have thought about it much or considered the danger to herself. And undercover work of any kind was dangerous. Her little foray into Alston's world proved that. "And the feminist in you couldn't say no?"

"There was no reason to say no."

"How about you putting your butt on the line while they sit back a safe distance and watch? Who are they? Feebs?"

"And Immigration."

A double-team. Great. "And you're definitely doing this?"

"I told them I needed to think about it. No point in looking too eager, but yeah." She stood. "I'm out of here. There are a few things I need to get in order." As she passed him, she patted his shoulder. "Take care of yourself, Drew."

Watching her walk away, Drew frowned. "Right back atcha." But he knew his words were wasted. She would do whatever she had to in order to bring down their target. That's what bothered him most—calculating the lengths to which Zaria would allow herself to go. But at least she'd deigned to confide in him what she was up to. In the scheme of things, that counted for something. Or maybe she figured he'd pester her until she spit it out and saved herself the bother. Either way, he didn't intend to take it sitting on his big behind.

With some effort he made it into Schraft's office. His head was down as he scanned papers on his desk. The rim of graying hair made a perfect inverted *C* on his balding head. Drew rapped his cane on the doorjamb to get his attention.

"I know you're there," Schraft said without looking up. "But you're not supposed to be."

"I'm not supposed to do a lot of things."

Schraft did look up then. "What do you want, Grissom?"

"You're not really considering letting her get mixed up in this thing, are you?"

Schraft sat back, rested his elbows on the arms of his chair and folded his hands. "Give me one reason why I shouldn't."

"For one thing, why aren't their own investigators working on it?"

"She's got an in. She knows the target." Schraft sighed. "I might have tried talking her out of it if I hadn't already gotten word to play along."

"So what the higher-ups want is more important than protecting your own people." Drew ground his teeth together. He knew that was the way it was, despite what he'd said to Schraft. But he didn't like it.

"I don't like it, either. But you're wasting your breath with me. If Zaria had said no, I would have backed her. The lady is who you have to convince."

"Tried that."

Schraft gave him a look that asked what else Drew expected of him. Damned if he knew. He only knew his gut was telling him that Zaria was putting herself in danger once again, and unnecessarily this time. Besides, he didn't trust the Feds to have her back the way he or any of their team would. They'd press her to get what they wanted without caring too much how she did it since she wasn't one of their own.

To Schraft he said, "I think I'll be taking a couple of days off after all."

For that he was treated to an eagle-eyed glare that told him Schraft wasn't fooled. So what?

"Keep your nose out of where it doesn't belong," Schraft said, but without any conviction.

Drew winked at him. It wasn't his nose anybody had to worry about.

Chapter 5

Facing her bed, Zaria surveyed the array of clothing she'd spread out across it with satisfaction. Usually she dressed conservatively in jeans and button-down shirts for work, and classic separates for anything else. For what she was about to do she needed a whole other wardrobe, something to attract Jimmy's attention and suggest that whatever she was up to wasn't on the up-and-up.

She'd only been home ten minutes when she'd called the number Gonzales had given her and told him she would do it. He wasn't surprised to hear from her, but he'd seemed pleased she'd agreed. He'd laid out exactly how he wanted to introduce her into Jimmy's world and what security he would provide for her, since wearing a wire of any kind might kill the thing before it even began.

Naturally they wanted to get her inserted as soon as possible, before she had a chance to change her mind. Not that she would. She knew how these things worked. They'd find desperate, unsuspecting women eager to get to the States, most of whom couldn't afford the exorbitant passage fees, telling them they could work it off once they got here.

What they didn't tell them was that they'd be working it off on their backs or that they'd find some pretext or other under which the women could never get from under their financial grasp. The girls ended up used up or dead. Though she was no big fan of folks simply skipping over the border illegally, she found it deplorable how ready some were to exploit dreams of American freedom and prosperity harbored by these young women. She would do what she could to put a stop to it.

The sound of the doorbell ringing ended her musings. When she looked through the peephole it didn't entirely surprise her to see Drew on the other side of the door. She'd known this afternoon he hadn't run through the totality of his objections to this assignment. That's why she'd left. She hadn't figured he'd follow her home to finish voicing them.

She pulled the door open, fastening a glare on him that usually felled lesser mortals. "Before you say anything, I'm warning you, don't start." She stood aside to let him enter.

He seemed unfazed by her words or her glare. "The least you could do is offer a guy a place to sit down." He hobbled over to her sofa and flopped onto one of the cushions with an exaggerated groan.

Zaria rolled her eyes, not buying his feeble act. She perched on the arm of one of the adjoining chairs. "What do you want, Drew, aside from a comfortable spot to rest your backside?"

"Are you sure you really want to go through with this thing?"

In some ways, she thought he'd be the last one to question her motives. He knew how hard she'd worked, even to get where she was now. She wouldn't do anything to jeopardize her plans, nor did she act in a foolhardy manner. She took chances sometimes, sure, but she didn't have any death wish. She knew what she was doing, and she wished he understood that. It would be nice for a change to have someone believe in her.

"Yes, I'm sure I want to go through with it. I wouldn't have agreed if I didn't. What bothers you more—that I'm involved or that you aren't?"

"Both."

Well, there was a truthful answer for you. "What can you do that I can't?"

"Watch your back while those scumbags are watching everything else."

Was that his real objection—that the men she'd work with wouldn't protect her properly? "Agent Gonzales assured me that they'll have men watching me at all times when I'm with him."

Drew's expression said what he thought about that. Not much. "What does Harry think of your doing this?"

That was Drew's nickname for Harrison, which he couldn't manage to say without a note of derision in his voice. Just like a man to think another man would help him bring a woman in line. "Harry's gone, and even if he weren't, do you honestly think I'd let him tell me what to do?"

"Guess not." He sighed in a way that suggested he'd given up, but she wasn't fooled. "When do you go in?"

For a moment she debated telling him anything, then decided what the hell. It might appease his sense of masculine protectiveness if he thought he knew something. "Acevedo owns a social club off Webster. I'll be going there tonight."

"Viva Boriqua."

"Something like that." Like her, Acevedo's ancestors hailed from Puerto Rico and his club catered to that crowd.

Drew rose to his feet. "I'd better leave you to get ready."

She watched him as he walked toward the door, his earlier hobble nowhere in evidence. He was up to something, she was sure of it, which made her regret what little she'd told him. She followed him to the door. "Don't you dare try to mess this up for me," she warned him.

He affected a wounded look. "How could you think that about me when I only have your best interests at heart?"

She huffed out a breath. He was laying it on a bit thick, but she didn't really believe he'd do anything to stand in her way. In truth, she appreciated his concern. She didn't have anyone else knocking on her door wondering if the path she'd chosen was a wise one.

She studied his face. From the first time she'd met him she'd considered him a handsome man, with warm brown eyes and a pair of dimples that appeared when he was amused, both incongruous in such a rugged face. He was the only man she knew who could make her feel short at five feet eleven inches tall in her stocking feet, as she was now. She would never have considered getting anything going with him. For one thing, she wasn't his type. He preferred the more vapid sort of beauty that would put up with his bullshit. For another, they worked together and even if she didn't have a rule against that the NYPD did.

As much as he teased her, he'd never earnestly tried to get anything going with her, either. But the bear hug he threw her way was new. For a moment she closed her eyes and drank in the warmth of his big body.

He pulled away almost immediately. "Take care of yourself, Zaria," he said, then let himself out the door.

She stared after him a minute before closing the door. What had that last bit been about? And why did that simple touch leave her feeling flushed? She shut the door and went back to her bedroom. She didn't have any time to waste wondering what he was up to. She had a date tonight and it wasn't with a fellow cop named Drew.

True to their word, Agents Gonzales and Spenser arrived at her apartment at eight o'clock. By the time they arrived, Zaria had settled on a red dress with spaghetti straps and a tight bodice and flared skirt as her first meet-and-greet ensemble. Her legs were bare but her feet were encased in a pair of T-strap pumps that fit her comfortably enough to dance in should the situation call for it.

Both men eyed her critically when she opened the door, but only Gonzales spoke. *"Muy guapa,"* he remarked.

"Thanks," she said, in response to Gonzales's compliment on her appearance. She knew a major part of the deal would be attracting Acevedo's attention as a man. A man would confess more to a woman he hoped to conquer or one he thought was his faster than some junior high school acquaintance. Their knowledge of each other was the in; keeping his interest was the real task at hand.

Once they were all settled in her living room, Gonzales produced a series of photographs and spread them out on her coffee table. "This is the inside of the club." He pointed to one photograph. "Here's the bar at one corner of the room."

The picture showed a pretty standard wood bar with a mirror behind it. A Puerto Rican flag hung above the bartender's head, along with the words *Viva Boriqua*. Drew hadn't been far off after all.

"Here's the dance floor." Gonzales pointed to another photo.

In this one she could see not only the dance area but the circular tables covered in white tablecloths that ringed the area.

"Acevedo has an office upstairs from which he can watch the comings and goings." Gonzales pointed to another picture showing a broad set of windows obscured by vertical blinds.

"That's if he's there," Zaria countered. "How do you know he'll be there tonight?"

"He's there every Friday night."

If they said so. But all this reminded her that they'd done some serious surveillance on the man before they ever got her into the picture. If that were true, how come they couldn't make anything stick? That was a question for another time, she supposed, returning her attention to the pictures the men showed her.

"What's this?" she asked, pointing to a door that bore the sign Private Use Only. A burly bald-headed man appeared to be standing guard in front of it.

"Those stairs lead up to the office."

That explained the burly bodyguard. "Is there anything else I should know before going in?"

"Watch yourself. We'll have a man at the bar and another couple at the tables. But we won't be able to do anything for you if he takes you upstairs. Try to keep it on the main level for tonight if you can."

She nodded. "Let's do it, then."

Gonzales cleared his throat, looking like he wanted to say something, probably to give her one last chance to back out. She wasn't having any of that. "Look, you asked for me. You got me. I'm not looking for an out."

Despite what was wise, she felt eager to get going. Her professional obligation wasn't the only reason. She'd spent part of the afternoon looking through old photo albums and couldn't find one clue as to why the skinny, awkward kid she'd known in junior high school would turn out to be someone two government agencies would want to bring down. As far as she knew, he'd gotten away from the old neighborhood, away from the crime and the drugs and the police sirens at all hours of the night. What brought him back, seeking to exploit his own people, or as close to it as you could get?

As much as part of her wished he were innocent, another part of her doubted he could be. She'd spent another portion of the afternoon checking him out on the Internet. Ostensibly, he was a businessman who did a lot of fund-raising for charity and political causes, a do-gooder. In Zaria's experience, that much clean often hid a whole lot of dirty. Either way, she intended to find out and do what was needed accordingly.

She stood and reached for her handbag and shawl. *"Vamonos, muchachos."*

"There's one more thing," Spenser said, rising. He pulled a tiny evening purse from his pocket. "We need you to carry this."

Chapter 6

Drew stood at the bar in the Nuestra Vida social club nursing a glass of Scotch while he waited for Zaria to appear. According to the bartender, the place didn't really get jumping until ten or eleven. In the meantime, the sparse crowd wasn't providing him much cover. At his size, nothing short of a Sherman tank would, but he hoped Zaria wouldn't spot him right off and do something uncalled for, like telling him to go home.

Truthfully, he just wanted to satisfy himself that the Feds or whoever else took proper precautions to protect her. He'd already spotted one guy at one of the tables that looked squirrelly enough to be a Feeb. There was another guy a few feet down from him at the bar who bore a similar look. Was that it? What were these two guys going to do if she really got herself in trouble? As it was, they were all lucky there were no metal detectors at the door or they'd all have been screwed.

Drew spotted her then, standing at the entranceway, surveying the club. He hunched down, hoping the guy next to him shielded his face though he could still see her. Damn, she looked good. He didn't think he'd ever seen her in a dress before. Not one that clung to her curves and ended way above her knees. She crossed the floor to one of the empty tables facing Acevedo's office and draped her shawl against the back of her chair. He wondered if she were carrying, considering she probably couldn't fit more than a lipstick in the tiny purse she had with her. He only hoped she'd come here armed with more than a pretty smile.

It didn't take more than a minute for the first guy to come up to her. He slid into the seat next to her like a snake slithering up to a juicy mouse. Drew had no idea what she said to him, but he slunk away after a few minutes. Good. She didn't need any distractions and neither did he. He didn't want to have to blow his cover by dragging some horny idiot off her.

Soon the club started to fill. A movement in the room upstairs drew his attention. The blinds had been drawn open. A man in a dark suit stood near the glass, looking down. Drew recognized him as Acevedo, though he liked to go by the name Jaime now, according to the Web sites he'd visited.

He moved away from the window almost immediately. A few seconds later, Acevedo and two other men, obviously bodyguards, came through a door on one side of the club. He made his way through the crowd, shaking hands and kissing faces. The man had the schmoozing technique of a politician.

Drew's gaze slid to Zaria. She must not have missed Acevedo's entrance into the room, either, since her gaze seemed glued to him. Acevedo must have noticed her, too, since he began walking in her direction. Drew downed the remains from his glass. Now the fun would begin.

Zaria noticed the moment Jimmy recognized her. There was a little pause in his step as he walked across the floor that she doubted anyone but she recognized. He pivoted in her direction. The scenario she'd discussed with Gonzales included treating this like a coincidental meeting, if it happened at all. But if he'd recognized her so immediately, it made sense that she should recognize him, too.

She knew they were listening, thanks to the tiny transponder sewn into the lining of the purse she carried. The powers that be must have changed their minds at the last minute about having her miked. It didn't matter. What were they going to do? Burst in and tell her to stick with the story as planned?

Jimmy stopped in front of her table. "I think I know you," he said, loud enough to be heard over the music. "You used to be Zaria Bennett, didn't you? Two pigtails," he added, gesturing.

"Still am. And you used to be Jimmy Vega. Skinny, glasses, obsessed with frogs."

"Only *el coquí*," he said referring to a species of frog indigenous to Puerto Rico. He slid into the seat beside her. "It's so good to see you. You haven't changed a bit."

"You have," she said in a way that implied feminine appreciation. "It's good to see you, too."

"I have some people to see to, but I hope you'll join me upstairs for a drink later. For old time's sake."

She nodded. "For old time's sake."

He bent and kissed her hand before leaving. Whoever had gotten hold of Jimmy Vega had definitely laid on the smooth lessons good. She wasn't buying it, though. There was something disingenuous about him that she couldn't put her finger on yet, but she would.

She sipped the rum and Coke she'd ordered, wondering what Drew thought of her meeting with Jimmy. She hoped he didn't think he'd succeeded at hiding his presence from her. Damn that man. She'd told him not to mess this up for her and he'd better content himself watching her from the bar.

She took another sip of her drink and set it on the table. As she sat back she saw a man approaching her. She recognized him from one of the photos Gonzales showed her—the burly bouncer. "Mr. Acevedo sent me to ask you if you're ready to join him."

Zaria nodded. Jimmy must have gotten rid of whoever he'd had in his office pretty quickly, which meant he was interested. Good. She collected her purse and shawl and followed the man to the back of the room.

The guard held the door for her. "It's just up the stairs."

The guard wasn't following? That meant Jimmy wanted to be alone with her. Even better. When she reached the landing she took a deep breath for courage, then rounded the corner through another door and into his office. It was a typical masculine space with dark wood and burgundy leather furniture. A host of diplomas and awards were posted on one wall next to a bookcase filled with hardcover volumes. She wondered if they were meant to impress, like the awards, or if he'd actually bothered to read any of those books.

Jimmy, who'd been seated on the sofa on the opposite wall from the window, stood as she entered. "Come in," he called to her.

She forced a smile to her lips and stepped forward. She sat in the spot he indicated and crossed her legs.

"*¿Quieres* champagne?"

Considering that the bottle he lifted from the ice bucket bore the Cristal label, she'd love some. "Sure." One didn't afford such luxuries on a cop's salary. He filled two glasses. When he handed one to her she clinked it with his. "To old friends."

"To old friends," he echoed.

As she drank she could see him watching her in the periphery of her vision. There was nothing friendly in the unguarded gaze he sent her way. That look was about avidity and lust, and it pleased her. "Can I make a little confession?"

"Does it have to do with me?"

Egotist. "In a way. I came here hoping I'd see you." She let her words hang there, waiting to gauge his reaction.

"Oh?"

She lifted one shoulder in a feminine shrug. "I've been out of the city so long. I thought it would be nice to see a friendly face."

"And you thought of me?"

"Most of the people we used to know moved away."

"Or are incarcerated or dead. Sad to say, a pretty typical story."

She said nothing to that. Only a law enforcement officer or someone trying too hard to impress ever said the word *incarcerated.*

They reminisced for a while about people and places they'd known. It would have been easy to forget during those few moments that she was undercover and he was her mark. Again, she wondered what, if anything, had happened to shift Jimmy's life so far out of focus.

Jimmy leaned back against the sofa, draping his arm across the back of it. His hand lightly touched her shoulder. "So, what have you been up to all these years?" he asked.

She leaned closer to his caress. "A little of this, a little of that. I was on the West Coast for a while," she said, being deliberately evasive. If he wanted to check her out, he'd have nothing much to go on. At the same time, she didn't make whatever she'd been doing sound completely on the up-and-up. Let him stew in that if he wanted to. Besides, she'd done what she came to do. She'd baited the hook. Now it was time to see if he'd really bite.

She set her glass down on the table. "It's getting late. I should go."

"Have dinner with me. Tomorrow night."

And they had a nibble. "For old time's sake?"

"No."

She fastened an assessing gaze on him. "All right." They made plans to meet at an Italian restaurant the next evening.

When she reached the first floor she did a quick scan of the room, searching for Drew. He wasn't where she'd last spotted him or anywhere else she could see. For all she knew he'd taken that inopportune moment to go to the men's room and would miss her departure. Good for him. He could stay in there all night waiting for her to come down, for all she cared.

Gonzales and Spenser were supposed to be waiting for her in a car around the block. She hurried toward the corner, since her shawl offered little protection against the chilly October air.

Reaching the car, she slid into the back passenger seat and shut the door a moment before the car pulled off. As before, Spenser was driving. Undoubtedly, they'd both listened to what went on between her and Jimmy. From the expression on Gonzales's face, he wasn't pleased.

"When exactly did we decide you'd gone there to meet Acevedo?" he said, his jaw tight.

"*We* didn't. Once I saw him face-to-face I didn't think he'd buy the coincidental meeting thing. I made a judgment call."

"I thought we agreed you would stay on the main floor."

"We agreed I would try to stay there, but I saw an opportunity and I took it. He wants to see me again. Isn't that what you wanted?"

"Yes, but—"

"When it comes to switching the play, you're no innocents,

either. We agreed I wouldn't be miked, then you hand me this."
Zaria opened the purse, let the solitary lipstick it contained fall
to her lap, then tossed the purse to Gonzales.

Gonzales's expression soured. "That couldn't be helped."

Which probably meant someone higher up than either of
them had called that shot. "Wishing you hadn't gotten me
involved in your investigation now?"

"Of course not," Gonzales said in a conciliatory voice. "In
the future, stick to what we agree upon."

She wasn't making any promises about that. "I'm going to
need some sort of cover story that goes deeper than 'a little of
this and a little of that.' I'm meeting him for dinner tomorrow."

"We know. We'll have something for you tomorrow morning."

"All right." The car pulled to a stop in front of her building.
"Good night, gentlemen."

She got out of the car and used her key to open the front door.
She paused a moment to make sure it closed behind her. Just as
she heard the click, a pair of hands grabbed her, one around her
waist and the other hand clasped around her mouth to prevent
her from screaming.

A stomp on her attacker's instep, an elbow to the stomach and
a second later she had her weapon out, shoved up under the
man's jaw. Breathing heavily, she blinked up at him. Damn. She
should have known all along. She pushed away from him,
lowering her weapon, though the urge to shoot him anyway
assailed her. "What do you want now, Drew?"

He had the nerve to grin at her. "Welcome back from the ball,
Cinderella. How'd you make out with the prince?"

Chapter 7

Zaria took a step away from him. "That is *so* not funny right now."

He couldn't help that. It was two in the morning, well past time for both him and his funny bone to be in bed. At least he had his answer now as to whether she'd been armed, though with that little peashooter she carried, the only way it would be of any help was to use it the way she'd done on him. Though he sure didn't mind watching her tuck it back where she'd got it from— a holster between her thighs.

When she looked back at him, he scanned her face. She looked even more weary than he felt. He wondered if that was due to the late hour or something else. "Seriously, how did it go?"

She folded her arms in front of her, eyeing him with a combination of disbelief and annoyance. "However it went, couldn't you have waited until I got to my apartment and knocked on the door, or, better yet, called me at a decent hour in the morning?"

He shook his head. "If you left Frick and Frack alone in your apartment for five seconds I can guarantee you your walls would have a new set of ears."

From her expression he gathered she hadn't thought of that. "More good news." She sighed. "I repeat, what do you want that couldn't have waited until tomorrow?"

"I wanted to see how you were doing."

"What, couldn't you tell from your spot at the bar?"

"You noticed that, huh?"

"It was like watching an elephant trying to hide behind a rose bush. Was that really necessary?"

"I told you I planned to have your back. We're part of a team, that's what we're supposed to do for each other."

"We're a team, huh? Funny, I don't see any members of that team here but you. Why is that?"

For an instant he contemplated telling her that he'd made the mistake of letting her get to him. He could imagine her reaction to that. If she didn't laugh outright, she'd swear he'd lost his mind. "You don't really want to know, so don't ask me."

She gave an exasperated sigh. "Fine. Whatever. It's late and I'm going to bed."

She turned to walk away from him, but he pulled her back with a hand on her arm. "Just one more thing. While you were busy playing footsie with Heckle and Jeckle, I checked out the story they gave you. Whoever torched that place didn't do so to cover up the murders. There was no chance of that. From what I hear, the girl with the slit throat was an immigration agent who got burned. The gunner used the commotion to try to escape. The madam got whacked for letting it all go down on her watch. The fire was to hide evidence of whatever else was going on there. If Acevedo is involved in this, the man is no joke."

"I know."

He cupped her chin and stroked his thumb over her cheek. "Sweet dreams, then." He turned to leave. He was about to open the door when she called to him.

"Hey, Drew."

He glanced at her over his shoulder. "Yeah?"

She was watching him with her arms folded and her head cocked to one side. "Thanks."

"All in a day's work, baby," he drawled. "All in a day's work."

Zaria let herself into her apartment, dropped her keys on the table and headed to her bedroom without bothering to turn on a light. Aside from being scared half to death by Drew, she was tired from the late hour and irritated to realize Heckle and Jeckle, as Drew called them, had lied to her. They'd told her that neither one of the younger women had been identified. That couldn't possibly be true if one of them was an agent. Damn. What else were the two of them keeping from her to get her to cooperate?

Whatever it was, she'd have to puzzle it out tomorrow. She stripped and slid under her covers nude. Scratchy was already asleep on his pillow. She rubbed his back and was rewarded with a deep purr. When had it come to this—that the most agreeable male she knew happened to be a cat she didn't want in the first place?

She shut her eyes. Figuring that out would have to wait, too.

The next morning, Zaria dressed in her usual manner. She intended to go into the station, but she had another task to see to first. The drive was over in half an hour. She stopped at the front desk and flashed her driver's license at the attendant at the desk. "I'm here to see Rosario Fuentes."

The young woman smiled at her. "Please sign in. I'll let her know you're here."

As usual, her grandmother was sitting beside one of the windows in the dayroom when Zaria approached. Instead of seeing her grandmother's characteristic welcoming smile, her face bore a worried expression. "*Que pasa, m'ijita. ¿Tienes un problema?*" Rosario asked as Zaria bent to kiss her hello.

Zaria usually visited on Sundays. It hadn't occurred to her that a day-early visit would cause her grandmother to worry. Zaria slid into the seat next to her grandmother. "*Todo está bueno.* I just wanted to talk to you."

That seemed to mollify her grandmother somewhat. "What about?" Rosario made a point of trying to look at her hands. "No ring yet?"

"No, *Abuela.* No ring." She held up her left hand for verification. The likelihood of receiving one was much less now than it was the last time she'd seen her grandmother since she'd given Harry the boot. Her grandmother didn't need to know that, though.

"*Entonces,* what did you want to talk to me about?"

Zaria let out a sigh, giving herself one last moment to debate bringing her grandmother into this, especially since she might not remember anything. But the chance was worth it. In her search to uncover information on Jimmy, there was precious little about him, save for the assertion he'd grown up in the Fordham section of the Bronx. What happened after that was decidedly sketchy. She knew the women in the old neighborhood had gossiped among themselves. Maybe her grandmother had heard something back then.

"*Abuela,* do you remember this friend of mine from junior high school? He went by the name Jimmy Vega then."

Rosario frowned. "I don't remember him so much, but the mother. *La chica esa,*" she said in derision—that one. "She thought she was so hot. She got some man to buy her a house in the suburbs. A businessman. Ha. Funny business. *Las drogas, las putas*. That's the business he was in. Everybody knew it but her. And once he got her out there, he beat her and her son. Him I felt sorry for. *Era un niño chulo*."

He was a sweet kid. Zaria had thought the same thing about him. But her grandmother's revelations changed things. Enduring the beatings of a cruel stepfather, a man involved in illegal activities, just as he was coming into his own manhood could have had a profound effect on him. "How do you know all this?"

"She ran away from him once. Just her. She left the kid with him. He came and dragged her back. I never saw any of them again." Rosario scanned her face. "What does any of this have to do with you?"

"Jimmy's under investigation for possible links to prostitution and drugs."

"As they say, the apple doesn't fall too far from the tree, eh, *m'jita. Tenga cuidado*."

She kissed her grandmother's cheek. "I'm always careful."

Rosario's skeptical look told her how little she believed that. "*Mira, niña*, men don't want to marry women with more ambition than sex appeal."

Zaria stood. "Then let's hope I have enough of each to go around."

Drew knew the minute he'd stepped outside his truck that he'd picked the wrong moment to stretch his legs. Under normal circumstances, he'd have stayed inside the vehicle, but his leg was still sore from the day before. That would have been fine, except Zaria picked that moment to step out of the facility. She'd spotted him immediately, too. Now she was walking toward him with a purpose in her stride that boded trouble.

She stomped to a stop when she reached him. "What, are you stalking me now?" she demanded.

If he'd realized she'd be coming here when she left the house this morning, he'd have gone home and gotten at least a couple hours of sleep. He'd spent the night watching her apartment in case she got any unexpected visitors besides him. That hadn't been his plan when he'd showed up on her doorstep last night, but considering her new buddies hadn't seen fit to watch her, he'd taken up the slack.

"How's grandma?"

"Fine. She didn't ask about you."

He leaned his back against the side of the truck and folded his arms. "Low blow, Zee. I'm only doing what Heckle and Jeckle should be. How do they know Acevedo doesn't have someone trailing you?"

She gave an exasperated sigh. "It seems Jimmy's life took a turn for the worse, not better, once he got out of the neighborhood."

He listened as she recounted what her grandmother told her, not completely surprised by the information. If Acevedo had gone bad there had to be some explanation for it. He might have made it out of the old neighborhood, but not every move proved to be a good one. He thought of his own childhood, after Jackson had come to live with him. His mother had done the obligatory thing, taking Jackson in after he'd been orphaned by his father's death, but she'd made Jackson pay at every possible turn for the inconvenience.

Drew had done his best to shield his younger cousin, even taking responsibility for some things he had no part in. It didn't matter, as Vivian Grissom had been determined to blame Jackson for whatever she could, including stuff he didn't do. Drew had never been able to find an excuse for his mother's behavior. Some people, both men and women, just didn't need to be parents.

"What do you plan to do now?"

"I'm heading into the house. Gonzales and Spenser have some sort of cover story to lay on me. How about you?"

"Get some sleep, I guess. I want to be fresh for our date tonight."

"Drew…" Zaria warned, then appeared to give up on that line of conversation. "Try to be a little less conspicuous this time."

"I'll see what I can do."

Chapter 8

Zaria arrived at the precinct to find that the team hadn't gone out that day. With Drew taking a day off, her being late and Bruno in court, there wasn't much of a team to send out.

Zaria took a deep breath and headed for the office. She'd been wondering what sort of background they were going to invent for her. It had to be something that would provide her an entrée into Jimmy's world—a past that could be verified to some degree if anyone wanted to check.

After a brief knock on the door, she poked her head in. "Anybody looking for me?"

Schraft beckoned her with a wave of his wrist. "Come in. Have a seat."

She did as he suggested. She looked from Spenser, who stood with his back to the windows to her left, to Gonzales, who sat to her right. "What all did you boys come up with for me?"

Gonzales handed her a folder. "We figure Acevedo is down one madam after the Perez woman was killed. If he checks he'll find you ran a place in L.A. for a while. Look that over and let us know if you've got a problem with anything."

She opened the folder to reveal a photograph of an elegant-looking building with a red door and red awning proclaiming the Hollywood Spa. At least she hadn't been running a dive. Inside was information about the operation, the employees, the clientele and, most important, who she'd had to pay off in order to stay in business. Briefly she wondered how they'd gotten this information and what they had on whoever would vouch for her, but decided she didn't want to know.

She snapped the folder shut. "I'll tell you what I do have a problem with—you folks withholding information. The woman who got her throat slit wasn't some nameless hooker. She was one of yours." She pointed that last remark toward Gonzales.

To his credit, Gonzales didn't bother to look the least surprised at her assertion. "You see why we can't send someone else in. Acevedo is already suspicious."

Instead they'd send in someone he already knew, hoping to throw him off the idea he was being investigated. Or they hoped so. The Jimmy she knew wasn't that stupid. He'd suspect her, even though they claimed a shared past. It might be easy for him to believe that she hadn't taken a straight and narrow path considering the neighborhood in which they had grown up. Besides, dirty people always assumed everyone else was dirty; the trick was discovering what kind of dirt you had on you. She only hoped the cover story they'd provided for her would hold up.

"You want me to do your dirty work for you, fine. But I don't want any more surprises or you guys can crawl back to whatever holes you came out of 'cause I'm off this."

"Agreed."

That came from Spenser. She cast him a hard glare that made him look away. "I'm sorry if we weren't completely honest with you, Officer Fuentes. In our rush to get everything in place we may not have been as forthcoming as we should have been."

Right. She believed that like she believed in little men dressed in green with pots of gold. If she hadn't let it be known she knew the truth, they never would have told her. Come to think of it, what was the big rush to bring Acevedo down? If what they told her about the timing of the women's deaths was true, they'd occurred only days ago. Wouldn't they want to allow at least a little time for things to cool down before they started back up again?

"Why are you in such a hurry?"

The two men exchanged one of their enigmatic glances.

Gonzales said, "I think you would want to bring down someone preying on your own people."

That was a nonanswer, but probably the best she would get out of either of them. She was tempted to answer something flip, like they were only half her people since she was half Puerto Rican and then not even really that, since the women in question were from Mexico, not P.R. That was a quibbling difference, if any, so she didn't bother. She wasn't sure either man understood the concept of humor. They wanted what they wanted and that's all they cared about.

She gave it another try anyway. "I thought we weren't keeping secrets."

This time Spenser spoke, surprising her. "We have reason to believe there were other girls working for him. We don't know what happened to them."

Zaria wondered why they'd kept that information from her. If anything, Spenser's admission made her more certain that she wanted to see this thing through. Or maybe that was the point; they'd figured at some point she might need more motivation to cooperate. "You think Acevedo will lead you to them?"

"That's what we're hoping." Gonzales stood. "We'd better be going." He shook Schraft's hand. "Thanks again, Sergeant, for your cooperation."

Schraft, who'd been silent the whole time, didn't bother to stand, but he did shake Gonzales's hand. "Anytime."

After the men cleared out, Schraft turned to her. "I'd understand if you wanted out of this."

In other words he'd back her if she wanted to back out. "No. I'm in, for the time being, at least." Truthfully, Spenser's admission made her more certain that she wanted to see it though. Besides, she knew she'd cause Schraft considerable trouble if she backed out at this point without a solid reason to do so. Depending on how tonight went, she might not have much choice in the matter. Once she stuck her neck out she'd have to see it through. She'd bet that's what the men who'd just left were counting on.

"Then I want you out of your apartment. If anyone followed you, it would be too easy to trace you back here. I'm assuming your legal name is on the lease, the mailbox."

It was. Then it occurred to her that Schraft had expected her to back out. That's why he hadn't said anything in front of the others. He'd expected her role in their investigation to be over so there would be no need to move her. If he thought that, he didn't know her very well, did he?

Schraft slid one of his cards toward her. "The address is on the back."

Zaria recognized the place as one of the luxury apartment buildings along the Bronx River Parkway on the Bronx-Westchester border. "Nice digs."

"Make sure they stay that way. The department is footing the bill."

Which meant that Schraft had put his butt on the line arranging it. "Thank you." She stood. "I'd better get settled in before tonight."

"If you need anything, let me know."

"I will." She let herself out of the office. It occurred to her that a side benefit to the move was that her new agent friends wouldn't know where to find her unless she told them. She'd have to consider giving them a heads-up a lot of thought.

The only person Zaria considered calling was Drew, and only because she didn't want him camped outside her apartment. He'd told her he planned to go to bed, but for all she knew she'd find him in bed with some woman not opposed to nooners. But when he answered the phone his voice sounded rough, as if he'd just woken up.

"It's me," she said in answer to his gruff hello. "I just wanted to let you know I'll be moving."

"What?" She heard the muffled sounds of sheets rustling. "Where are you going?"

"Schraft arranged for an apartment for me. I just wanted you to know."

"Don't go anywhere until I get there."

The line went dead before she had a chance to protest. Damn. She hadn't intended for him to do anything. In part, she'd told him so that he'd know a level of protection had been added to her safety so he wouldn't worry or whatever it was that had prompted him to get involved. The last thing she'd expected was for him to come over.

Well, she had bigger things to worry about. She went to her bedroom to pack her wardrobe and gather the personal items she would need. Scratchy sat on the bed, alternately watching and licking his paws. She'd have to leave him with her neighbor since there was no point in taking him. She didn't know if she'd be around enough to take care of him.

She rubbed a spot between the cat's ears. "Sorry, buddy, but I can't take you with me this time." Scratchy put his head down as if he were disappointed.

She'd almost finished packing when her doorbell sounded, the one upstairs, not the buzzer for the door downstairs. "How do you keep getting in here without being buzzed?" she asked Drew when she opened the door to him.

"Trade secret. Are you ready to go?"

"Almost. I have to get the litter box."

"When did you get a cat?"

"I didn't. He sort of adopted me and I couldn't refuse."

"Sounds familiar. The not being able to refuse part."

She supposed that was a slam on her accepting her current assignment. "I know you manage not to do anything you don't want to do, but some of the rest of us aren't so cavalier."

He cast her a sour look; she wasn't sure why. "At least they've done something right, moving you."

"That was Schraft's idea."

"Why does that not surprise me?"

Zaria sighed. "My bag is in the bedroom." She hoped that would put an end to the conversation. Not only did she not like its direction, but on the chance Drew was right about her apartment being bugged, a possibility he seemed to either have forgotten about or didn't care about, she'd rather not have the men listening to what they thought of them.

Drew went to claim her bag. She took Scratchy next door to her neighbor's house. The older woman had volunteered to watch him whenever Zaria needed. Something told her that the cat would be having a better time of the next few days than she would.

Chapter 9

Stepping over the threshold of the apartment, Zaria let out a high-pitched whistle. From what she could see, the whole place, from fuzzy carpet to the textured ceiling, was pristine white. Even the furniture was white. Not the regular stuff you could find at IKEA, but antique pieces. The kitchen was to the right, but beyond that the apartment opened into a large living room. On the other side was a hallway that she assumed led to the bedroom. Despite the starkness of the color scheme, the place struck Zaria as a very feminine space. "One of these days, I'm going to have to ask Schraft who he keeps in this place."

"Someone with a high tolerance for snow blindness," Drew replied.

"Come in," she said.

"Nah, I've got something to take care of. I just wanted to make sure you got where you were going." He winked at her. "Catch you later."

She watched him as he strode out the door. There was something different about him, though she couldn't place her finger on it. Maybe he'd whacked his head on the concrete harder than she'd thought. But it had started before then. She couldn't say the exact moment she'd noticed it, but it was definitely before then.

She shut the door. She had more important things to think

about than the vagaries of Drew Grissom's behavior. She got the file Gonzales had given her out of her bag and read it over until she had the information memorized. She didn't know if she would have to use it, but better to be prepared now than sorry later.

"What is it this time, Grissom?" Schraft said when Drew appeared at his office door that afternoon.

"Tell me you're happy with the way this thing is playing out with Zaria and I'll go now."

Schraft fastened him with a hard look, the purpose of which Drew couldn't begin to guess. Maybe the sarge wanted to see if he'd go away easily. But it would take more than a single glare for that. After a moment, Schraft let out a harassed sigh. "I can't. What do you want me to do about that?"

"She needs someone on the inside with her looking out for her interests."

Schraft eyed him for a moment. "What exactly do you suggest?"

"Assign me to work on the case. I'll drive her."

"You're actually asking me?"

The note of incredulity in Schraft's voice annoyed him. Drew had never minded other cops thinking whatever they wanted to about him, but Schraft should know better. Drew might not have the greatest respect for authority, but he'd never ridden over any of Schraft's orders without at least telling him what he intended to do first. But since his goal wasn't to antagonize Schraft but to get him to cooperate, he didn't bother to point that out. In a somber voice, he simply said, "Yes."

Schraft leaned back in his chair and steepled his fingers, an indication that he was considering it. Drew knew he would. It was an arrangement easily explained that would put him on the periphery of whatever she was up to. With his size, everyone would probably assume he served the dual purpose of providing muscle. Either way, he'd be looked on as someone inconsequential, not worthy of much scrutiny.

Schraft made a noncommittal gesture with his shoulders. "I think it could work."

That's about as excited as he expected Schraft to get about the idea. "So do I."

"I'll have to let Gonzales and Spenser know about the change in plans."

A feral grin spread across Drew's face. "No, please. Let me."

That night, when Zaria opened the door to him, her surprise was written on her face. "What are you doing here? I've got to leave any minute."

"I know," he said, walking past her into the apartment. When he reached the living room, he stopped and turned to face her. "I'll be driving you."

Her brow furrowed. "You? I just spoke to Gonzales fifteen minutes ago. He didn't mention that."

"He doesn't know. Schraft put me on it."

"*Schraft* did? Somehow I find that hard to believe. What's going on, Drew?"

He hadn't expected resistance from her and was unprepared for it. Luckily, he was saved from having to respond when the doorbell sounded.

Zaria frowned and headed back toward the door. He took that opportunity to move farther into the apartment. He took up a spot in one corner of the sofa and waited for the men to come inside.

Not surprisingly, neither man looked happy to see him. Gonzales in particular had a puss on that was close to a pout. "What's he doing here?" Gonzales demanded.

Gonzales had been speaking to Zaria, but Drew took pleasure in answering. "I'm Ms. Bennett's new driver."

"Says who?"

"It's a condition of Ms. Fuentes's continued cooperation in this investigation. Ask Schraft if you don't believe me." Schraft hadn't exactly said that, but Drew didn't mind embellishing. He took out his cell phone and offered it to Gonzales. "Call him yourself."

Gonzales cast him a sour look, then turned back to Zaria. "Did you know about this?"

"I knew it was being considered. The decision wasn't made until this evening."

Drew smiled and put his phone away. At least Zaria wasn't willing to rat him out in front of the others. He knew she'd check with Schraft even if the others didn't—and she'd do it before they left. That was fine with him. He knew once Schraft made a decision it stayed made.

"That's fine," Spenser said, in a voice that suggested he didn't want to quibble. Drew could get to like that guy. "Zaria, did you look over the material we gave you?"

"Of course."

Spenser asked her a few questions designed to see what she remembered. Zaria answered without hesitation, and in a way that seemed to satisfy Spenser, at least. Gonzales still had the puss on. While Drew wondered about that, he didn't care too much, either.

Zaria, who'd been sitting on the matching love seat across from him, stood. "If you gentlemen will excuse me, I need to freshen up before we go." She headed toward the back of the apartment without waiting for any of them to respond.

Drew gave her enough time to have called Schraft before he followed. He found her in the bedroom perched on the edge of the circular bed, still talking on her cell phone. The room looked like something out of *Arabian Nights,* with filmy white cloth hanging at the windows and around the bed. Schraft was really going to have some explaining to do one of these days.

He rested his shoulder against the doorjamb, waiting for her to hang up. She glanced up at him, an annoyed look on her face. "All right," she said into the phone. "I'll fill you in tomorrow." She clicked the phone closed then looked up at him. "That was Schraft."

"I figured."

"Funny, he doesn't recall your conversation this afternoon exactly as you do."

Drew shrugged. "Why didn't you rat me out to your friends out there?" He nodded in the direction of the living room.

"Aren't you the one who said members of a team are supposed to stick together?"

He had. He hadn't expected she'd paid any attention to it, though. He also doubted that was her sole reason for doing so.

Since he doubted she'd be more forthcoming if he pressed her, he decided to let it slide. "Are you ready?"

She rose to her feet. "As I'll ever be, I guess. How do I look?"

Drew inhaled. She wore a two-piece black sleeveless dress. Both parts clung to her in a way that left nothing to the imagination. "Fine."

She looked at him oddly, as if she were trying to figure something out. Then she shook her head, picked up her cell phone and put it into her purse.

She shook her head again, then slipped past him out the door. For the first time, she seemed distracted, which Drew didn't like. Zaria would need all her brainpower focused on Acevedo if she was going to pull this off. At least he'd have a few minutes in the car to make sure her head was together. If it wasn't, he'd drive off and he didn't care what anyone had to say about that.

At the curb, Zaria eyed the big black Mercedes parked in front of her building. Since Drew was driving she figured he'd been the one to secure the car. She looked up at him as he held the back door open for her to get in. "Where'd you get the wheels?"

"I borrowed them from a friend."

She sat and pulled her legs in. "A friend?"

He nodded and shut the door behind her.

She watched him as he rounded the car and got in behind the wheel. She knew the department kept a few luxury vehicles seized from criminals for their undercovers to use, but if that was where Drew had gotten the car, he would have said so. As far as she knew Drew didn't know anyone with the financial means to lend him such a pricey automobile, with the possible exception of his cousin, Jackson. Although Jackson was a cop, his wife was head of one of the most successful black cosmetic companies in the country.

"You mean this is your cousin's car?"

He started the motor. "Who, Jackson? No."

He pulled away from the curb. He was just going to leave her guessing? Then a thought occurred to her. "You don't mean borrowed like you'd better have it back before morning when the owner gets up to go to work, do you?"

He grinned at her over his shoulder. "Of course not." He stopped at a light. "If you must know, Jared Naughton lent it to me."

She blinked. Jared Naughton as in the film director Jared Naughton? "You know Jared Naughton?"

"Long story."

"I've got time."

"A couple of summers ago Jack and Carly got themselves in some trouble on Martha's Vineyard. They were up there shooting a commercial for Carly's cosmetic company."

"The ones with Samantha Hathaway?" she asked. Actress Sam Hathaway had recently been voted one of the 100 Most Beautiful Women in America by one of the entertainment magazines. "You know Samantha Hathaway?"

"Kinda."

Zaria shook her head. She'd known Drew for almost three years and had no idea what lofty circles he'd traveled in. She supposed it wasn't exactly station-house conversation, but it surprised her. What else about him didn't she know? She'd already been questioning a shift she'd detected in him, making her question what she thought she knew about him. She still couldn't put her finger on it, but she knew she wasn't imagining it.

She sighed, running her fingers over the soft leather upholstery. Whatever Drew's problem was, she couldn't focus on that now. Figuring out another man's machinations was much more important. She needed to have her mind focused on that. She glanced out the window. Another couple of blocks and they would be there.

Drew pulled to a stop outside the restaurant. She waited until he came around the car to hand her out.

"Are you sure you're ready for this?" he asked as she joined him on the curb.

"Of course," she said to him. She adjusted the cape she wore around her shoulders as she looked up at the restaurant's festive decor. To herself she whispered, "Showtime."

Chapter 10

Zaria had planned her entrance to be fifteen minutes after their appointed meeting time. There was no point in looking over-eager, and it gave the agents watching Jimmy a few minutes to observe him without her present. Before they left the apartment, Gonzales had told her to expect a pair of agents to be dining at another table. As the hostess escorted her to the table where Jimmy already waited, she spotted the couple almost immediately. Her guess was that they were trying to pass for lovers, but she had more chemistry with her building super than these two appeared to have with each other.

Determined to ignore them, and any other prying eyes around the restaurant, she stopped when the hostess arrived at their table. Jimmy had already claimed the seat facing the door, which left her the chair facing the interior.

"Sorry to be late," she said in a voice that suggested she really wasn't.

Jimmy was already on his feet. "I'm just glad you could make it." He moved around the table to seat her. As he did, Zaria noted for the first time that he was shorter than she, or at least shorter than she was in three-inch heels. She wondered if he'd noticed, too, but he didn't say anything. Then again, he seemed too busy drinking in every inch of her. She'd worn the outfit as a distraction, but it annoyed her to see how easily he'd taken the bait.

Jimmy slid into his seat. "You look—" He paused as if he couldn't find a word to complete his sentence. His gaze settled on her cleavage. "Incredible," he said finally.

Slimy son of a bitch. She brought a seductive smile to her lips. "Thank you. You don't look too bad yourself."

"Who, me?" He tugged on the lapels of his jacket. "Underneath this I'm still that skinny kid from *el barrio*."

She doubted that. Even if he were simply a businessman as he claimed, she'd bet he'd done a few things the Jimmy she'd known wouldn't have dreamed of. The waitress appeared to take their drink orders. Zaria asked for a glass of white wine, Jimmy a sweet vermouth on the rocks.

"Sweet vermouth?" she asked, surprised at his choice of drink.

He shrugged. "I figured when in Rome…" He gestured in a way that encompassed the room.

Zaria took the opportunity to scan the dining crowd. Aside from them and the two diners in the corner, the clientele looked like they'd escaped from the set of *The Sopranos*. Zaria had wondered at his choice of restaurant when he'd suggested it. She would have figured him to be more at home with a place that served rice and beans and platanos than pasta and braciole—someplace he'd be welcomed as a big man to impress her.

Now she understood why he'd brought her to the place in the shade of Arthur Avenue, the Bronx's equivalent of Little Italy. He wanted someplace where he could be anonymous, for what purpose she couldn't as yet gather. For the time being she'd play along and see what developed.

She leaned her forearms on the table, folded her hands and sat forward. If he wanted to stare at her cleavage, she'd give him an excellent view. "I hate to tell you, but I don't think vermouth is the drink of choice anymore. I think that died out with old man Mazetti," she said, referring to an older man who'd lived in their neighborhood, who mourned the passing of his wife with a daily bottle of the liquor.

The waitress brought their drinks and took their dinner order. After she left, Jimmy lifted his glass. "To old man Mazetti, then."

She clinked her glass with his before taking a sip. For a house wine, the vintage was pretty good. "Not bad." She set her glass on the table.

In that short time, Jimmy had drained his glass. "Tell me about you, Zaria. What have you been doing in L.A. these last three years?"

Zaria scanned his face before answering. She'd told him she'd been on the coast for a while, but she hadn't mentioned L.A. and she certainly hadn't mentioned a time frame. Was this his way of letting her know he'd checked up on her or was he unaware of what he'd said? By the calculated look on his face, she'd have to pick the former. That was fine with her. She'd rather deal with him on a business level than try to ingratiate herself as a paramour. But judging from the lustful way he watched her, he'd probably be greedy and want both.

"I was a sort of office manager for a business out there."

"What made you want to come back?"

The story was that the spa had been raided and shut down. She could have told him some variant of that, but she didn't want to play her hand too soon. She shrugged. "Can any New Yorker really get used to all that sunshine? I wanted a white Christmas for a change. Besides, my grandmother is in a place here."

"Which one, *la negra o la Latina?*"

The black one or the Hispanic. She knew what he wanted to hear. Some people only deemed to be concerned with or wish well folks like themselves. If it hadn't been the truth she would have lied, anyway. "*La Latina.* It got to be too much of a hassle to visit."

He seemed to accept that. "You know my mom passed when we were young."

As she understood it, that death had most likely come by his stepfather's hand. "I was sorry to hear that."

A waiter came to deposit a basket of bread and bread sticks on their table. Jimmy pushed aside the cloth napkin, offering her first choice of the bread inside. She picked a doughy bread stick but didn't bother to butter it. She broke a piece off and popped it into her mouth. The bread was warm, soft and delicious.

Jimmy picked a roll. As he buttered it, he said, "Why don't you ask your friend to join us?"

"Excuse me?" she said, surprised.

"The big black guy at the bar. He's been staring at us the last ten minutes."

Zaria looked over her shoulder to see Drew, who lifted his glass to her in salute. Damn him. They hadn't discussed what he'd be doing while she was inside. She hadn't thought it necessary. But she supposed this was his way of inserting himself into the fray. She'd get him for that.

She turned back to Jimmy. "He's not my friend. He's my driver."

"Looks like he does a bit more than drive." He touched the side of his head at the same spot where Drew's stitches were still visible.

"A girl's got to be careful these days."

"No doubt. But while I appreciate his vigilance, I'd prefer to eat my dinner without two eyes boring a hole in me."

He was asking her to make a choice, albeit a small one. That's how folks sucked you in—they asked you to make little concessions and the next thing you knew they had you hooked. She didn't mind letting him think he'd won a small victory. "Excuse me."

She walked over to where Drew half sat, half leaned on one of the bar stools, letting her hips sway, knowing Jimmy was watching her. But her eyes were on Drew, really looking at him for the first time that night. He wore all black from the mock turtleneck under his jacket to the shoes on his feet. He really did have that dark and dangerous thing going on, if a girl was into that.

The gaze he settled on her was one of sexual familiarity, which obviously they didn't share. He wondered if that look was for Jimmy's sake, and if it was, if Jimmy could even make it out over the distance.

She drew to a halt inches away from him. "What the hell do you think you're doing?"

"I thought I was having a drink."

"He wants you to go."

A feral grin spread across his face. "Does he?"

She ground her teeth together. "Yes, he does. So do I. Now go."

"Fine." He tossed back the remains in his glass and stood. "I'll be with the car."

When she turned to walk back to the table, Jimmy was talking on his cell phone. If she wasn't mistaken, he was probably on the line to someone outside telling them to watch what car Drew got into so that he could get the license-plate number. That's why she figured he wanted Drew out of there in the first place. Too bad. If she knew Drew, the plates on the car were fakes that would lead them nowhere.

As she slid into her seat, Jimmy flicked the phone closed. "Sorry. A business call that couldn't be helped."

Zaria shrugged. In the meantime the waitress had also delivered their entrées. She'd ordered chicken in a carbonara sauce. For a moment they ate in silence. She kept a pleasant expression on her face, knowing he watched her.

After a while he wiped his mouth with his napkin and set it on the table. "What do you want from me, Zaria?"

She picked up her glass, twirling its contents. "What makes you think I want anything?"

"Everybody wants something."

"Maybe I just want to renew an old acquaintance."

His look turned skeptical. "We were never that close."

In her mind, they had been. He'd been picked on for being short and geeky in a world where machismo ruled. She'd been teased for being tall and unfeminine in a world where daintiness was appreciated. They'd been each other's only friend. In her world that counted for something, but obviously not in his. But if that's the way he wanted it, she could play it that way, too.

"I've been looking to set myself up in something here in New York. A girl's got to eat."

"And you thought I could help you with that?"

"Or you might know someone who could. I assumed a man of your stature would be able to reach out a helping hand."

"There are other more conventional means of making money."

So he knew how she'd supposedly made a living. "I can't keep my grandmother in Pine Forest flipping burgers." She was barely ekeing it out now. But she'd given him a motivation for why she'd chosen the life she had, which would hopefully help her case.

He remained silent a moment, tracing a pattern on the table-cloth with his index finger. "What if I could help you? What would be in it for me?"

"What do you want?"

His gaze lowered from her face to her cleavage and back, though he said nothing.

Son of a bitch. She hadn't been expecting any other answer, but it still stung to realize how far this former friend of hers had sunk. She let a sensual smile form on her lips. "We'll have to see how you do."

He tipped his head, a smile of challenge on his face. "Yes, we will."

The waitress approached their table to ask if everything was all right. Jimmy gestured in a way that indicated they were finished. *"¿Quieres café?"* he asked her.

No, she didn't want any coffee. She wanted to get out of there as quickly as possible, while her skin hadn't managed to crawl off her bones yet. There was no reason to stay. He hadn't made her any promises and he wasn't going to. He'd given her nothing but innuendo. Depending how you read their conversation he'd proved nothing more than that he was a horny man on the make.

He had to decide if he trusted her, and she doubted anything she said now would convince him of that. And the longer she stayed, the more likely he'd want a sample of what she'd promised. After seeing him tonight, she was willing to do whatever it took to get him, but the longer she could put that off, the better.

"No, gracias," she told him. She took her napkin from her lap and placed it on the table. "I'd better be going." She stood. "Thanks for dinner. I hope I hear from you. Soon."

She walked away from him, keeping her pace as slow and seductive as she could manage. She claimed her cape and headed outside. The night was chillier than she remembered, or maybe it was the chill she felt inside her.

Drew was leaning against the car, talking to another man who'd probably come outside for a smoke considering there was a cigarette in his hand. Drew eyed her critically, but said nothing as she breezed past him to stand by the back door of the car. He beeped the lock and she got in without waiting for him to open the door for her.

A moment later, he slid in behind the wheel, then turned to look back at her. "You okay back there?"

"I'm fine." She gathered her cape more tightly around her. "Do you think you could turn on the heat?"

Chapter 11

Drew pulled away from the curb. He had no choice but to take Zaria at her word that she was all right, unless he wanted to press the matter, which he didn't. He couldn't imagine what that bastard had said to her in the short time he hadn't been watching to cause this shift in her mood. It was probably best he didn't know, since his most likely reaction to whatever it was would be to go pulverize Acevedo and think about the consequences later.

He switched on the heater and was rewarded with a blast of cold air. He flicked it off. He'd try again in a moment. "So how did it go?"

"Exactly as I expected it to. He's done some checking on me. So far he knows what I was supposedly up to in L.A. He may be willing to help set me up here, for a price."

"What's that?"

"Sleeping with me. What else?"

Over Drew's dead and bullet-ridden body. "You're not seriously considering that."

"If that's what it comes to. I'll have to bone up on my faking technique."

He appreciated her attempt at humor, even if it fell flat. It meant she'd gotten over whatever emotion had driven her out of the restaurant in such a hurry. He still wondered about it, though. "So what made you hightail it out of there so fast?"

She sighed. "I don't know. I think I was still hoping that it was all a mistake. If you'd known him as a kid, you wouldn't believe he could turn out like this. He was a marshmallow. I was glad when he moved, because sooner or later the neighborhood would have eaten him alive. I thought he was better off."

Drew could testify that a better environment didn't necessarily mean a better life. He'd grown up in the suburbs with good schools and all that, but his childhood had still sucked since his mother had been such a bitter woman. Dealing with her had shaped his outward persona since he was determined to never let her see that anything she did got to him.

He said to Zaria, "So you don't believe he mistakenly got into this mess."

"He's dirty some way. Why else would he bother to find out about me?"

That was Drew's take on it, too. He turned onto the street that housed her new apartment. Before he got halfway up the block he noticed Gonzales's car double-parked in front of the building. Good God, how much of a jackass could this guy be? Drew hadn't mentioned it to Zaria, but they'd had a tail since they left the restaurant. He hadn't tried to lose the guy since doing so might seem suspicious, and as far as he knew they weren't trying to keep her location a secret. But if Gonzales was stupid enough to be sitting outside her building that changed things.

"Do you have Gonzales's cell-phone number?" he asked Zaria.

"Yes. Why?"

"Call him and hand me the phone."

She did as he asked, though he knew she had to be curious as to what he was up to. When Gonzales picked up, Drew said, "This is Grissom. Drive off."

Gonzales sputtered. "What are you talking about?"

"Drive off, now. I'll explain later." The other car's headlights came on and he could hear the sound of the engine coming to life over the phone. "Call me back in fifteen minutes."

He closed the phone and tossed it onto the seat beside him. As the other car moved off, Drew pulled into a parking spot across the street. The car that had been following them drove past, but stopped farther down the street.

"Do you mind telling me what all that was about?"

"I'm sure one of Acevedo's guys was following us. He's still here, a little farther down with the blinkers on."

"Checking out the home turf?"

"That's my guess. Wait for me to come around."

She did as he asked, but she ignored the hand he offered her to help her out. Drew supposed she'd have to hand in her Tough Cookie medal if she actually accepted any help from him graciously. But she didn't object as he placed an arm around her waist as they crossed the street. He supposed he should be grateful for small favors.

Once inside the apartment, Zaria took off her cape and draped it on the arm of the sofa. "Do you think we should call Gonzales?"

"Nah, he'll call back." And when he did he'd get Zaria's voice mail, since Drew had deliberately left the phone on the front seat of the car.

"Then you entertain the boys for a while. I'm going to take a shower."

"The boys" showed up ten minutes later. Zaria had yet to emerge from the bedroom, so Drew answered the door.

"What the hell was that about?" Gonzales demanded, stalking past Drew into the apartment. Spenser, wisely, said nothing.

Drew closed the door behind the two men, then went to the living room. "Where'd you two pick up your training, the Floyd Kenyatta School of Beauty? Didn't it occur to you to maybe lie low until she got home instead of double-parking what is clearly an unmarked car in front of her building?"

"Why should that matter?"

For the love of God. "We had a friend see us home. I haven't checked, but for all I know he's still waiting down at the end of the block."

"Oh," Gonzales said. Spenser shrugged, looking as exasperated as Drew felt, making him wonder what the arrangement was between the two men. Of the two of them, Gonzales seemed to have more juice on the investigation, though Spenser seemed to have more sense. How had that come about?

"Where's Officer Fuentes?" That came from Spenser.

"She's changing. She should be out any minute." She should have been out already. Remembering how she'd come out of the restaurant, he was tempted to go find her to make sure she was all right. Instead he claimed the same corner of the sofa he'd occupied earlier. If she needed time to regroup, he'd make sure she got it.

Gonzales went to check the living room window while Spenser joined him on the sofa. "How'd it go at the restaurant? Did Acevedo give anything up?"

"Not much. He let it be known he'd checked up on her. I hope whatever story you've concocted holds up."

"It will."

Looking over at Gonzales, Drew asked, "What's his story?"

Spenser's gaze followed the direction of Drew's. "Another time." He pulled out a card and handed it to Drew. A cell-phone number was written in red ink at the bottom of the card. "Use it if you need to."

Drew understood why Spenser wouldn't elaborate now. With his deep voice, whispering wasn't exactly an option. Drew tucked the card into the breast pocket of his jacket a moment before Zaria made her entrance to the room. She wore a T-shirt over a pair of low-slung sweatpants and a pair of fuzzy slippers. Her hair was damp and her face was devoid of makeup. He supposed he had his answer as to what had taken her so long.

"Sorry to keep you guys waiting," she said.

"Not a problem," Spenser said. He stood to allow Zaria to sit, then took a place on the love seat. "Officer Grissom started to fill us in."

"Is there anything else you need to know?"

Gonzales wandered into the room and stood behind the love seat like a specter. "How did you leave it?"

"He's supposed to call me if he's got something for me."

Spenser stood. "Call us if he contacts you. We'll arrange a meeting place if necessary. We can see ourselves out."

After the men left, Drew turned to Zaria. She'd pulled her legs up under her and rested her elbow on the back of the sofa, facing him. He touched his hand to her thigh. "I should be going, too."

"I guess. Sure you don't want to hang around and open the bottle of wine I bought this afternoon?"

Sure he would, but that was a temptation he couldn't afford to give in to. He'd been telling himself he needed to get his head together, but having seen Zaria dressed the way she was before hadn't done anything to cool his libido. Even now, with no makeup and her hair in a ponytail, she was still sexy as hell. "Some of us have to go to work in the morning." He removed his hand from her thigh. "Walk me to the door."

She nodded. "All right." She preceded him into the hallway. She paused with her hand on the doorknob. "Sure I can't get you to change your mind?"

If she kept looking at him with that siren's smile on her lips, maybe. But he'd only be torturing himself. He brushed his knuckles across her cheek. "Get some sleep." When she loosened her grip on the doorknob, he opened the door and stepped into the hallway. He waited until he heard the sound of the locks turning before heading toward the stairs to go down to his car.

After locking the door, Zaria leaned her back against it and sighed. Things were bad when you couldn't get party-boy Drew to hang with you. Rather than being tired, she felt enervated— exhausted but too hepped up to sleep. Besides, it was only ten-thirty. For some people, the night was just starting.

And then it occurred to her what was different about Drew. He'd left without any comments about her looks or ribald comments about why she wanted him to stay. He wasn't like that with every woman, but he was with her. It was how she knew he wasn't serious about anything he said. It was a teasing relationship she enjoyed since it helped break up the monotony of the job while they waited for something mind-blowingly dangerous to happen.

But lately she'd seen none of that from him, aside from the morning two days ago. The only explanation that came to her mind was that something was going on with him that he hadn't told her about. That wouldn't be too surprising since they didn't tell each other everything. Still, it did concern her. She liked Drew and she didn't relish the idea of someone hurting him or treating him badly. Despite her ragging him sometimes about his unorthodox attitude, she trusted him with her life.

The only thing she doubted was that it was a woman. To her

knowledge, Drew had never let any woman in too close. He'd been married once and joked that the only way another woman would get him to the altar again was hog-tied with an apple in his mouth. Given his size, that would not be an easy task. Well, she hoped it wasn't a woman, partly because his change in attitude would suggest that there was strife not harmony between them. The other part of that was an odd brand of jealousy. He was one of the few people she considered her friend. Him becoming involved with someone in a serious way might change that. Or maybe it already had. Maybe that's what this new Drew was about, him distancing himself from her so as not to cause a problem with his new woman.

Zaria pushed off the door. She was just making stuff up now, trying to come up with a motive without a real clue. There was no point in speculating. She'd do what she always did when she wanted to know something from him; she'd ask him. He probably hadn't gotten home yet. While she waited an appropriate length of time, she looked for her cell phone. Then she remembered Drew had taken it from her in the car. She used the house phone to dial his home number and got the answering machine. She waited a couple more minutes, then tried his cell.

"Grissom," he said when he picked up the phone.

"Where are you? I called your house a minute ago."

"What's up?"

"You didn't happen to leave my cell phone in the car, did you?"

"I have it here. I'll drop it by in the morning. Anything else?"

Zaria inhaled. "Yeah. Is something going on with you that you haven't told me?"

"Like what?"

"I don't know. You tell me. You've been…different lately. Is everything okay?"

He chuckled. "I'm cool."

Somehow she didn't believe that. Neither one of them said anything for a moment, then Drew came back with, "Can I ask you a personal question?"

He was actually asking? Now she knew there was something wrong with him. Usually he just blurted things out and dealt with the repercussions later. "Sure."

"What happened with Harry?"

Though that wasn't the last question she expected, it surprised her. "It wasn't a good fit."

After the words were out of her mouth she realized the easy double entendre Drew could make of that comment. But none came. Instead he asked, "Why?"

She shrugged. She couldn't give him a precise answer. "After a while it gets easier for a girl to tell when she's picked a dud."

He chuckled again, a rich, throaty sound that made her smile. "I'll see you in the morning, then."

She switched off the phone and put it back in the cradle. Well, that had gotten her nowhere. She was left with believing that either she was imagining things or whatever his problem was he preferred to keep it to himself, and she doubted she was imagining anything. She'd have to live with that. If he got around to wanting to share she'd be there for him. But for tonight, she'd have to go to bed still wondering what it was.

Drew tossed his cell phone onto the passenger seat beside him and looked up at Zaria's building. The light in the living room went out a few seconds before the bedroom light turned on. She was going to bed. He pictured her there on that circular bed, amid all that gossamer fabric, and groaned. He'd have to develop a different line of thought or this was going to be a very uncomfortable night.

He shifted, tilting the seat back a little more. He could still make out both her apartment and any activity on the street, so he relaxed. The windows were tinted dark enough that no one could see through. He didn't trust Acevedo not to pull some stunt now that he knew where she was. Since Hewey and Dewey didn't see fit to look out for her, he would.

The light in her bedroom went out. Despite having asked him to stay, she must be tired. Fatigue pulled at him, too, but he was used to that. He'd spent more than a couple of nights awake thinking about her, wondering if he should make his change in feelings known then deciding against it. But she'd noticed the change in him anyway. He'd had the chance to tell her and he hadn't taken it, not only because that was something best done in person, not on the phone, but because she didn't need to be thinking about him right now. She needed to be thinking about the case.

Oh, who was he kidding? As much as they joked around together, Zaria was a serious woman. She knew what she wanted, or she thought she did. Drew Grissom didn't fit into that picture. That's what he'd been telling himself, anyway. If she wanted him, he was right here for the taking and she'd never given him any indication that she wanted anything more from him than his friendship.

Come to think of it, he'd never given her any reason to believe he wanted more, either. Knowing her, she would have taken any advance from him as being motivated by sex only, which wasn't the case. He appreciated her ambition, even if he didn't understand the single-mindedness of it. She was a compassionate woman, loyal to her family and those she considered her friends. He understood now that part of the reason she'd taken the case was an effort to prove her friend was innocent, and her disappointment now that she believed he wasn't. If he didn't watch it, he'd find himself even deeper down this rabbit hole he'd fallen into.

Or maybe it was time to take his shot or shut up about it. He'd watched her date a string of men who were not suited for her, saying nothing. He understood her desire for stability. That's what had brought him to his one incredibly bad marriage—the desire to have someone, anyone, love him without constant critique or judgment. That had been missing from his home life the same way a level of constancy had been missing from hers. But sometimes getting what you thought you wanted wasn't quite what you expected, as he'd found out firsthand.

Maybe it was time to find out if there really was something between them instead of driving himself crazy. He glanced up at her window. It might not be tomorrow, but soon, when this case was over and they were both thinking with clear heads.

Chapter 12

Around 4:00 a.m. Jackson showed up as Drew had asked him to. He needed a moment to get home, shower, shave and change clothes and didn't want to leave Zaria unprotected as he did so. Rather than switch parking places, they switched vehicles. After pointing out which apartment Zaria was in, he got into Jackson's car and drove home.

Stepping under the warm spray of the water, Drew groaned. His muscles ached after a night in his car. He leaned his forehead against the shower wall and closed his eyes. That was about all the rest he'd be getting for the foreseeable future.

He shaved and dressed, then headed back to Zaria's. He'd been gone only a little more than an hour, so it was still dark when he returned. He pulled up alongside the Mercedes, expecting Jackson to step out and reclaim his car, but he didn't.

Damn Jackson. If he was asleep in there, Drew was going to kill him. Usually Jackson was the responsible one of the two of them. He didn't dare honk the horn so he got out of the car and rapped on the driver's-side window. No response, and with the dark outside and the dark windows Drew couldn't see a damn thing. If Jackson was in there, he had to be dead to the world.

He went back to Jackson's car, found a parking space and headed up to Zaria's. The apartment was still dark, so as far as he knew, she could still be asleep. He wasn't going to take the chance of assuming everything was all right, though. He needed to see for himself.

He paused when he was about to knock on her door. He could hear voices on the other side, one masculine and one feminine. He assumed the woman was Zaria, but who was that with her? It could be Acevedo for all he knew. The voices didn't sound hostile. In fact, he'd swear he heard Zaria's laugh. No time like the present to find out.

He knocked on the door. When Zaria opened it, she was wearing the same outfit he'd seen her in last night. Her hair was in the same ponytail, but she had a new, sour expression on her face. "Come in, Drew. We were expecting you."

"We?"

"Your cousin has been telling me some interesting stories about you."

"He has?" He couldn't think of anything Jackson might tell her that would help his case any. Drew stepped farther into the apartment. The only light that appeared to be on came from the kitchen. No wonder he'd assumed she was still asleep, since the kitchen couldn't be seen from the street.

Jackson was seated at the small table at the other end of the room. "Hey," he said.

"Hey, yourself." Drew slid into the remaining seat across from him. "I thought you were supposed to wait in the car." He'd intended for Jackson to wait in the car. If he'd wanted Zaria to know he'd been watching her, he'd have told her himself.

"He would have," Zaria said, "if I hadn't noticed the car parked outside."

"She called me on the phone you left in the car and told me to come up."

Drew cast his cousin a narrow-eyed look. Jackson was enjoying himself way too much for Drew's liking. Drew supposed he deserved that. When Jackson and Carly were getting together, Drew had given him a tough way to go. But this wasn't the same situation. Drew had known almost from the beginning that Jackson and Carly belonged together, even if neither of them did.

"How did you know he was out there?" he asked Zaria.

"I didn't. I thought *you* were. Did you think I wasn't going to notice that car outside?"

He hadn't thought about it much, considering at no point had he seen her by one of the windows. "Why'd you wait so long to let me up?"

"I didn't intend to. I called to tell you that you were annoying me and to go home. When I found out it was Jackson, I let *him* up. I'm going to get dressed."

Drew turned to Jackson. Only then did he notice the empty plate in front of his cousin.

"She cooks a mean scrambled egg. You should have her make them for you sometime."

The grin on Jackson's face made Drew want to deck him. "Don't you have someplace to be?"

"As a matter of fact, I do. I'll tell Carly you said hi." Jackson stood and punched him on the shoulder. "Good luck."

Drew followed him to the door, locking it after him. Since Zaria hadn't returned he washed Jackson's dish and the few he found in the sink. That accomplished, he found a mug and poured himself some coffee from the urn on the counter. He was just settling on the sofa when Zaria reappeared. She'd changed into a pair of jeans and a T-shirt but she'd left her feet bare. The first words she said to him were, "Are you still here?"

She had to know that he wouldn't have left. She wanted to punish him for getting on her nerves. "Any chance the kitchen is still open?"

She sat on the other end of the sofa, drawing her knees up in front of her. "You are incredible, do you know that? And that is not a compliment."

He'd already gathered that she was ticked off at him. "What exactly did I do now?"

"I offered you the chance to stay up here and you declined. You'd rather skulk around in your car like I'm some civilian who needs a babysitter. You didn't notice anybody else down there, did you? Everyone else trusted me to take care of myself. Why not you?"

He didn't have an answer for that, since if she didn't see that everyone else had left her to the wolves, there was nothing he could say.

"No matter what anyone says, it's still harder for a woman to make her mark on this job. If a guy had been in my situation the other day, they'd be labeling him a hero. At the very least, they'd be looking to give him a commendation. What did I get for that? The punk-ass narc whose life I saved was pissed over being rescued by a girl."

He understood how she felt. The department wasn't exactly Neanderthal-free when it came to issues of race, gender or any other bias. "You know damn well that I trust you, Zaria."

"Do I? Then what have the last few days been about? So far you've nearly gotten yourself killed rushing into traffic, you followed me to my grandmother's place, you've insinuated yourself into the investigation I'm working on." She gestured in a way that invited him to comment.

"Maybe I don't want to see you get hurt."

"I rest my case." She unfolded her legs and stood. "Go home and get some rest, Drew. You look like hell." She walked off. A few seconds later he heard the sound of the bedroom door closing.

He sat there on the sofa, wondering if he should stay or do what she asked and leave. Why was she the only person on the planet capable of making him feel like he didn't know what he was doing? He should have told her. In the absence of any explanation she'd assumed his newfound overprotectiveness was a lack of faith in her.

Well, he couldn't sit on her couch all day. He went to the bedroom and knocked on the door. "I'm going. You want to come lock the door?"

When she opened the door, her irritated expression was gone. "Look, Drew, I was being cranky. I couldn't sleep last night, either. That's how I knew you were outside. You don't have to go."

Maybe it was best if he did, though. She didn't need him here and he could use the couple of hours of sleep she talked about. She was leaning against the doorjamb, her features soft. His gaze drifted to her mouth and the small smile resting there. He would go, but he wanted to get something straight with her first.

"You're not alone in this, Zaria."

"What are you talking about?"

"I know you want this guy. I want to help you get him. Since Schraft assigned me to this case, we are partners of a sort now."

"And?"

"And I don't want you putting yourself to any unnecessary risk."

Her eyes narrowed. "Is that so? Is this about what I said last night?"

In part it was, but not completely. But she didn't give him a chance to answer.

"Go home, Drew," she said, but there was no animosity in her tone. "You're starting to annoy me again."

At least she wasn't angry with him this time. He walked to the door with her behind him. Once there he turned to face her. "Give me a call if you hear from him."

"How will I know? You've still got my cell phone."

He fished it out of his pocket and handed it to her. "See you later."

He headed out to the car and got in. Looking up at the apartment, he shook his head. She didn't take him seriously on this, but she should. If it came to it, he'd step in to keep her safe.

Zaria shut the door behind Drew and let out a heavy sigh. Just like a man to obsess over what a woman planned to do with her body. She supposed it was her own fault for bringing it up in the first place. But it served to reinforce her notion that Drew thought of her as a woman first and a cop second. She didn't used to get that vibe off him, so when had that started?

Maybe she should tell him that she had no intention of letting it come to that. There were eight million ways to put off a guy who wanted to get in your pants. She knew how far to go before shutting him down without losing his interest. Any girl past the age of thirteen knew that.

She pushed off the door and headed for the shower. She wanted to be prepared if Jimmy called or came over. Drew hadn't told her about the tail last night until the last moment, but she'd figured it out for herself, long before he'd told Gonzales to drive off. She'd known by his vigilance in monitoring the rearview mirror that there was someone behind them worth noting. That was another thing she'd have to get him for later when this was done.

She stepped into the shower and let the water roll over her body. The only reason she wasn't more furious with Drew was that she kept something from him, too. She knew he didn't understand why she wanted this so badly, but she couldn't bring herself to tell him. She'd never told anyone about that night.

Her mind flashed to a time when she was a teenager, about a year after Jimmy left the neighborhood. It was a Saturday night, hot and humid, the air heavy with unspent rain. Summer nights in the neighborhood meant people congregated outside as long as possible since, without air-conditioning, which few could afford, their apartments were oppressively hot. As usual she was home with her grandmother. Outside was no place for a girl to be, as her grandmother used to tell her, despite the fact that the one fan they owned couldn't cool a flea.

The crowd outside was rowdy, which wasn't unusual. They'd been out all day, drinking beer, watching the kids play in the water from the fire hydrants. Every now and then the fire department would come by and shut them off, only to have some joker open them up again.

A sudden jump in the noise level outside had led her to the window. Down below, a man had a woman pinned beneath him on the hood of a car. Even at that young age, she knew what he was doing, right there, in the open, with everyone watching...not only people outside, but those at their windows. Not that any of them tried to stop him. If anything, they were egging him on, cheering, as if this girl's degradation had been arranged as a sport for their amusement.

Worse yet, Zaria knew this girl from her building. She'd seen her with this man, her supposed boyfriend, the week before. They'd been out on the stoop, him trying to cop a feel and her trying to fend him off. She wouldn't give him what he wanted and so he'd taken it in the most public and humiliating way possible.

Zaria swallowed, fighting the bile that rose in her throat. This was the place she'd lived in, where people acted no better than animals. She knew one thing then. She would get herself and her grandmother out of there as soon as she could. She didn't care how.

She felt her grandmother come up behind her. She'd been in

the kitchen watching dishes. Her warm, still-soapy hands gripped Zaria's shoulders as she leaned past Zaria to view the scene below. *"Dios mio,"* she said in a shocked voice that was almost a whisper.

Her grandmother stepped in front of her, blocking her view. *"Vaya al quarto, m'ijita. No es para tus ojos."*

Whether the scene outside was for her eyes or not, Zaria resisted being sent to her room, until it occurred to her that the window in there faced out onto the street, as well. She raced to her bedroom in time to hear her grandmother yell from the other window.

"¿Que tu haces abajo, Roberto? ¡Roberto!"

Everyone in the neighborhood knew her grandmother, and if she asked you what you were up to, you'd better tell her.

The man glanced upward. *"Nada, Mami. No es importante."*

Zaria swallowed. That's what he said, but even at that distance she could see fear in his eyes and his voice held a note of supplication.

"Deja esa chica solo ahora. Voy a llamar a la policia. Tengo el telefono acquí."

Zaria knew her grandmother would never call the police, whether he left the girl alone or not. No one she knew was a big fan of the cops. In this neighborhood the police were as unwelcome as they were in any poor area. Half the time, no matter what kind of call they showed up on, they'd be greeted by flying bottles or bricks. No wonder they didn't want to come over here and overreacted when they did.

But the threat must have been enough, or maybe it was the sound of encroaching sirens. A few minutes later she saw the telltale flashing lights approach. The man ran off, leaving the girl open and exposed. A policewoman pushed through the crowd, wrapped a blanket around the girl and led her away.

Zaria wondered at the bravery of that policewoman. The crowd could have turned on her. But maybe realization of what they'd been a party to crept in. People started slinking back to their own homes and for once the neighborhood was still.

Zaria swiped at her eyes. Every time she thought about that night it was with a profound sadness. A week later that girl had hanged herself from the shower in her family's apartment. But the tears surprised her. How long had it been since she'd cried over anything at all?

That night she'd learned something else about herself. She'd looked at that female cop and wanted to be her, wanted to be the one who provided safety and comfort in a crazy world. Now she was her, and if she could help it, Jaime Acevedo would never hurt anyone else again.

Chapter 13

It was a little before noon when the call from Jimmy came. "What are you doing this afternoon?" he asked when she answered the phone.

"Nothing I can't put off."

"Meet me at the Bronx Zoo in an hour. The main entrance."

"The zoo? Isn't it closed?"

"It's open year-round. A few of the animals are still out, the ones that like the cold. Besides, I'm a sucker for polar bears."

It seemed fitting he'd admire something capable of ripping a human being to shreds in seconds. "All right. But you'll have to feed me later."

"Not a problem. I'm looking forward to seeing you."

The line went dead before Zaria had a chance to comment. It was just as well, since she had nothing else to say. She dialed Drew's home number and waited for him to pick up.

"Grissom," he said in a sleepy voice.

"I'll give you three guesses who called me and the first two don't count."

"He wants to meet?"

"The Bronx Zoo of all places. Can you get me there in an hour?"

"I'll be right over."

Zaria hung up the phone and went to the closet to dress. She chose a long-sleeved red shirt that crisscrossed over her breasts, a short black skirt and high-heeled black boots. Hopefully they wouldn't do too much walking, or her feet would be unforgiving. Most of the time she dressed in flats, but she didn't want to give up her height advantage.

She contemplated calling Gonzales, but decided against it. His style of micromanagement was likely to get her killed. She'd let him know what happened after it went down, when he couldn't interfere.

Feeling anxious, she pulled on a fur jacket and went downstairs. Drew was pulling up by then. He whistled as he got out of the car and opened the door for her. That was the Drew she knew. She slid into the backseat and pulled her legs in. "You approve?"

"No, but if your goal is to make the man go nuts, you're hitting it."

Their drive was a short one, maybe ten minutes if they didn't hit any traffic. Maybe three minutes passed before Drew spoke. "What do you think he wants?"

Zaria shrugged. She figured it was another test of sorts. Men like Jimmy didn't expose themselves that easily, even to people they knew. It was her job to move him along the path to trusting her. "I guess we'll see when we get there."

"Did you call Gonzales?"

"What he doesn't know won't kill him."

"I guess I don't have to tell you to be careful."

They both knew that unless some unforeseen circumstance occurred he'd be waiting with the car, not following her. "Nope."

"Keep it short."

"If I can."

Drew sighed. "Put this in your pocket."

He handed her a cell phone. "Mine is charged."

"Yours doesn't transmit."

She shrugged and did as he asked. No wonder he wasn't fighting her about tagging along. He'd be listening the whole time. At least he told her about it rather than trying to plant something on her. Then again, he probably hadn't had time to slip into the precinct and "borrow" something better.

When they pulled into the main entrance there was another

car already parked. As Drew opened the door for her, Jimmy stepped out from behind the steering wheel of the other car.

"You look lovely, as ever," he told her when they both stood together by the car.

"Thank you." She allowed his kiss on the cheek. "Do you really intend to walk around in there? It's freezing out."

"I'll keep you warm." He linked his arm with hers. "There is something I want you to see."

She sighed as if she were resigning herself to her fate. She cast a look at Drew that told him to behave himself then allowed Jimmy to lead her through the entrance.

"What's so exciting at the zoo?"

"You'll see."

Considering that most of the cages were empty, she doubted the wildlife was high on his list of things to see. Apparently, they weren't on anyone else's list that day, either, since the place was virtually deserted. They walked along, arm in arm, talking about nothing in particular, looking to the few people they passed like a pair of lovers out for a Sunday-afternoon stroll. But what was the point? She wished he'd get down to business, whatever it was, but she couldn't afford to appear impatient.

Eventually, he led her to one of the large buildings. "The World of Darkness?"

He smiled in an indulgent way. "Don't tell me you're squeamish?"

Not in any way that counted. "Reptiles and scorpions and bats, oh, my."

He laughed as she expected him to. He gestured for her to precede him.

Once inside, it took a minute for her eyes to adjust to the darkness. They walked through, not paying the exhibits any attention. Finally, she stopped at an exhibit of snakes behind a glass window. It seemed fitting somehow and she was tired of this game. "Is this what you got me out here for? Bats and rattlers? Or is something else on your mind?"

He seemed pleased that she'd been the one to crack. A smile spread across his face as he backed her against the railing protecting the exhibit. His hand went to her waist beneath her jacket.

"I think I can help you, Zaria. Or someone I know can. How does that sound to you?"

She let a hint of a smile turn up her lips. "Keep talking."

"A friend of mine owns a club. The manager there needs to be replaced."

"What kind of club?"

"Strippers…" He trailed off in a way that suggested more was going on, which could possibly mean drugs as well as prostitution. That might be something, but she doubted anyone in their right mind would have kidnapped girls giving lap dances on the main floor. If they were there, they'd have to be in a back room somewhere.

She let her smile broaden into a seductive grin. "Sounds promising. When do I find out more?"

"Soon." His face was very close to hers and his hands came to life traveling upward over her rib cage. "Aren't you going to say thank you?"

She knew what he wanted. She would let him have this little victory, but only that. Cradling his face in her palms, she brought his mouth down to hers. She forced herself to respond as his tongue invaded her mouth and his lips ground against hers. She squeezed her eyes shut, trying to imagine herself with anyone else other than this man who revolted her. The only face that came to her mind was Drew's. Since she wasn't in a position to question what her subconscious conjured up, she went with it. It was Drew's mouth on hers, Drew's hands on her breasts, Drew's leg that had insinuated itself between her thighs. Never mind that Drew was back in the car listening to all of this. Damn.

Then Jimmy's hand gripped her hips, lifting her so that she sat on the railing. Both his legs were between hers now, his hands gripping her buttocks. If she let him, she knew he'd take her right here and now. No wonder he'd brought her here to a place that was secluded and deserted. Perversely, she wondered what turned him on more—the prospect of having her or having her here, where there was still the threat of discovery. *Freaking pervert.*

Either way, it didn't matter. She pushed back on his shoulders to get him off her. She was careful to make it seem like a playful gesture. "That's enough for you for today."

When he pulled back, he was breathing heavily, but there was a hard look in his eyes. "Don't tease me, Zaria."

She stared him right back. He'd said it himself. This was supposed to be a business arrangement. They weren't friends or lovers, no matter how they'd looked that day. "I'm not. You did partial work. You got partial payment." She pushed against him again, moving him backward enough for her to slide off the railing. "When I get the gig so will you."

She walked away from him, leaving him to follow or not. He did. He grasped her arm, pulling her back to face him. "Let's talk about it over that lunch you wanted."

She winked at him, knowing she still had him. "There you go."

Drew watched the pair of them return to the parking area, trying vainly to calm his temper. He wasn't exactly sure what had happened between them in those few seconds; all he'd heard was the audio. That had been enough. He remained where he was simply because he couldn't trust himself not to beat the ever-loving shit out of Acevedo if he got out of the car.

Since he knew where she was, he turned off the audio. He didn't need to hear any more. They stopped at the door to the car. Acevedo opened it and Zaria got inside. To him Acevedo said, "Do you know how to get to La Perla?"

Drew nodded, though he hadn't a clue. He figured Zaria would know. Once Acevedo closed the door, he pulled out into traffic. "Where are we going?"

She gave him rudimentary directions that would have to get more specific once they got closer. He eyed her in the rearview mirror. She was sitting directly behind him looking out the window. He wondered what she was thinking but didn't ask. By the faraway expression on her face he figured she needed a moment.

"Aren't you going to say anything?" she said finally.

Who, him? Not a word. "No."

"Not even a well-timed, 'I told you so'?"

But he couldn't seem to help himself. "What would you have done if he hadn't taken no for an answer?"

"I'd have kicked his ass. You know that."

And blown her cover in the process. "You're playing a dangerous game, Zaria. He's going to want more next time."

She sighed. "I know. But if you don't mind, let's change the subject. I'm trying really, really hard not to upchuck on the nice upholstery."

Drew ground his teeth together, not really sure who he was angry with. Acevedo for sure. The toss-up was between himself for letting her go off with him alone or Zaria for giving Acevedo at least part of what he wanted. As for the latter, hooking Acevedo either sexually or otherwise had been part of the game plan from the jump. He couldn't really blame Zaria for going with the program. If anyone had asked him, he'd have said it was a bonehead plan to start with, but no one had.

He'd known what she'd intended to do when she got out of the car, so he had no one to be angry with but himself. He knew the lengths to which she was willing to go. He wouldn't make that mistake again.

He found the restaurant without much trouble. He parked in the lot around the corner, cut the engine and shifted so that he could look at her. She had reapplied her lipstick and fixed her hair. "Listen, Zaria. There's a change in plans."

She cast him an arch look. "Says who?"

"Says me."

She shook her head. "Don't start with me, Drew."

"What if Acevedo had a reason to keep his hands to himself, at least for the time being?"

"What reason would that be?"

"That I might kill him."

She gave a scoffing laugh. "Why exactly is he going to be afraid of my chauffeur?"

Because given the first opportunity he would. "Let me work it out."

She gave an exasperated sigh. "Stay out of it, Drew." She got out of the car, slamming the door behind her.

Drew pulled out his cell phone, found the card Spenser had given him and called the number. Spenser picked up on the third ring. "What's going on?" he asked when he recognized Drew's voice on the phone.

"I'm outside this restaurant La Perla on Provost Avenue."
Drew didn't expect the man to know the location, only understand its import. "Zaria is inside with Acevedo."

"I thought you guys were supposed to call us if anything
happened."

"Yeah, well."

Spenser chuckled. "I know what you mean. Gonzales is a
good guy, don't get me wrong. He's dedicated, but he's new to
the game. Wouldn't know a decent investigation technique if it
bit him on the ass. Frankly, I'm surprised he was assigned to this
in the first place."

"Then what's he doing running the show?"

"It's their investigation. We got called in as a backup to assess
any danger to Homeland Security efforts. These people they
bring across the border, most are unsuspecting dupes, but the rest
are criminals. That's how it is these days. You can't start looking
into a crack in the sidewalk without the whole alphabet soup of
agencies wanting in."

"I hear you."

"What's the problem?"

"The whole damn setup is the problem, and the lady in
question has a case of tunnel vision as far as getting the guy."

"What do you suggest?"

Drew told him what he planned to do. Zaria wouldn't like it,
but she'd already told him she wouldn't go against him in front
of Acevedo.

"Do what you have to do," Spenser said. "I'll fix it from my end."

"Thanks."

Drew pocketed the cell phone and went into the restaurant. He'd
already seen them sitting at a booth by the window. He also knew
Zaria had seen him passing by. She wouldn't be surprised to see
him walk in. He slid into the booth beside her, draped his arm
around her shoulders and turned to Acevedo. "So, what did I
miss?"

Chapter 14

Drew had to hand it to Zaria. Aside from slightly stiffening when he sat down, she gave no indication that things were any different than she expected.

Acevedo, however, fastened on him a look of disdain. "We are having a private conversation."

In that moment, Drew realized Acevedo bought Zaria's story entirely and he was ticked because someone beneath him deigned to come where he wasn't invited. Maybe she'd played it right from the beginning, but he couldn't back down now.

He turned to Zaria, leaning over to whisper in her ear, "Baby, go powder your nose," but loud enough for Acevedo to hear.

For a moment, the expression on her face turned mutinous, which he expected. But he knew she'd do what he asked anyway. He slid out to let her pass. As she got out, she stepped on his foot with one of those spike heels. He retaliated by smacking her on the butt.

When he slid back into the booth, Acevedo said, "What do you want, Mr...." he trailed off, expecting Drew to fill in an answer.

He didn't. Instead he signaled the waitress to come over and ordered a cup of coffee. When she left, he rested his forearms on the table and clasped his hands. "I understand you and Zaria have got something going."

"What has that got to do with you?"

"Did you ever ask yourself what she was doing in California? She's a Bronx girl. She doesn't belong out there." He could see by the expression on Acevedo's face he hadn't. "She was hiding from me. She skipped town owing me money. She thought she could slink back in without me noticing."

"How much?"

He named a figure higher than he thought Acevedo could pull out of his pocket.

Acevedo frowned. "How does she owe you that much?"

"That's between her and me." He sat back as the waitress left the coffee. "Here's what you need to know. I don't mind a little fun in the monkey house if that's what you're into. But whatever it is you're going to do for her, do it quickly, 'cause until she gives me my money, that belongs to me."

He nodded over Acevedo's shoulder to Zaria, who picked that moment to return to the table. Damn if the girl didn't have perfect timing. Drew tossed a couple of dollars onto the table, more than enough to cover the coffee. He slid out of the booth in time to catch Zaria around the waist without breaking the momentum of her stride.

He expected her to explode at him the moment they were in the car, but she didn't. She stared out the window, her arms folded, her legs crossed. By the expression on her face, he couldn't tell what thoughts ran through her mind. "Aren't you going to say something?"

His question was met with continued silence. She didn't even turn to give him a dirty look. Damn. He parked and they went up to the apartment. She still hadn't spoken. He wondered what she was waiting for.

He had his answer once he turned back from locking the door behind him. She hauled back and punched him in the stomach. It hurt, but he knew she hadn't hit him as hard as she could have.

"That's for smacking me on the butt." She stalked off toward the living room. He knew that wasn't the uppermost concern on her mind. It was an excuse to whale on him. He followed her to the sofa, where she was leaned over unzipping her boots. "These things are killing me." She tossed the boots to the side.

"Is that all you want to say to me?"

She turned to him then, her anger showing in her eyes. "I had him, Drew. You know that. So what was that nonsense? What did you tell him, anyway?"

He couldn't argue with her assertion that Acevedo had bought her story so he didn't try. "I said that you owed me some money and that until you paid up he'd better keep his hands off you."

"And this helps how?"

For one thing he'd keep his hands off her. He'd seen that in Acevedo's face. He'd behave, until maybe he found a way to get Drew out of the picture. "Maybe he'll stop playing cat and mouse and get down to business."

She leaned back on the sofa, resting her head on the back. "This is just another example of you doing whatever you want."

That wasn't true, but he didn't want to argue about it. He leaned down, grasped her legs and pulled her feet into his lap. She didn't fight him, which was a plus. He took one of her feet in his hands and massaged the ball of it.

She sighed. "Oh God, that feels good." She shifted to get more comfortable. "Is that what you do to keep all those women of yours happy?"

He chuckled. There hadn't been anyone in a while, not since he started developing feelings for her. He took one of the small pillows for the sofa and slipped it under her feet. "Sometimes."

"Well, keep it up and I might actually forgive you."

He could tell by the tone of her voice she already had, at least as much as she intended to.

"You are explaining this to the suits," she continued.

"Spenser already knows."

"I see. So you really went behind my back."

"Zaria…" he started, not knowing where he'd end up.

She sat up, pulling her feet from his grasp. "Please, please don't explain any more. Not now. Since your little stunt deprived me of lunch, I'm starving." She stood and stepped over her boots. "Do you want something?"

His stomach rumbled, having been deprived of both lunch and the meal before it. "Sure."

"Stay there. I hope sandwiches are okay."

"Whatever." He was in no position to follow her, anyway. Having had any part of her nestled against him so intimately and hearing the little noises of contentment she'd made had elicited a predictable reaction. He'd pulled the pillow onto his lap more as camouflage for his burgeoning erection than as a cushion for her feet.

He didn't know why he bothered, since Zaria, as usual, was oblivious to his reaction to her. He didn't know why that bothered him so much, since he'd already decided to put his feelings on hold until after this was over, but it did. Maybe it was because she got such an easy bead on Acevedo, whom she hadn't seen in years, and had no clue when it came to him, Drew, whom she saw every day.

Or maybe she did. Maybe she did know and her withdrawal just now was designed to send him the message that she wasn't interested. Drew sighed. Now there was a possibility he didn't care to examine too much.

Jaime Acevedo stood at the window to his office, looking down on the action below. What had been a dance floor last night was now crowded with long tables and chairs and old ladies playing bingo. He had other places to be, other matters to attend to, but he preferred it here.

To the rest of the world he was a moderately successful businessman. Here, in the neighborhood, he was regarded as a hero. He'd given them a safe place for their kids to hang out in the afternoon, a haven for the old folks and a place to party. If anyone had a dispute they couldn't settle, rather than fight they came to him. Every time he turned around, the Spanish newspapers printed some flattering report of what he did. He wondered what all of them would think if they knew the sort of enterprises that funded his largesse.

A young woman working the floor came into his field of vision. Her height, jet-black hair and long legs reminded him of Zaria. He found himself hardening instantly. He didn't know why he wanted her so badly, but he did. She was from the old days, when he was nothing, an unwanted child born to a mother who couldn't begin to guess who'd fathered him. Skinny and awkward, he'd been picked on and harassed, the butt of too many jokes to count. Zaria had been his friend, but he'd known even she'd thought he was pretty lame. Maybe that's what drove his libido; she was the last thing from the old neighborhood left to conquer.

He pushed that thought from his mind. He was used to assuaging his desires, not examining them. But he admitted he had been surprised to see Zaria here that night. He'd expected her to be long gone. When he'd first come back to the Bronx, he'd asked around about her. All anyone seemed to know was that she'd gotten a job right after high school and moved away. He'd hoped her leaving proved more auspicious than his had been. He'd hated his stepfather, but the man had taught him one thing: if you wanted something, go after it and take it. That's what he'd done ever since.

But he guessed that wasn't the case for her, either. There was something about this neighborhood that got inside you, took root, tainted you regardless of your intentions. He didn't know how she'd let that man get his hooks in her, or if that really was the case. For all he knew, she was playing him for some reason he didn't fathom yet. He only knew the animosity he detected between them was real.

He was tempted to do Zaria a favor and just take the other man out. But he wouldn't do that, not yet. He didn't even know the man's name, much less what his business was or what repercussion there might be for him if he did what he wanted. He was too hot and couldn't afford any slip-ups right now, which included Zaria getting hurt in the process. He knew where they were and he could afford to wait.

In the meantime he'd string her along in a way that nothing could lead back to him. He could be a patient man when he needed to be. But sooner or later he'd get what he wanted. He'd make sure of that.

A knock sounded at the door. He checked his watch. Right on time. Roark had many vices, but tardiness wasn't one of them.

Roark was in his early forties but he had a craggy face that suggested he'd been stomping around on the earth much longer than that. "Hey, man," Roark said, offering his hand.

Acevedo shook his hand, saying nothing. He gestured toward the sofa.

When they were both seated, Roark said, "What did you want to see me about?"

Roark was all-business, too, which he appreciated. "You know your place by the highway? Have you found someone to run it yet?"

"Not yet. I was thinking of giving it to my sister. Why?"

"I might have someone for you. An old friend."

"How old?"

Acevedo chuckled. He doubted if Roark would have a problem if every woman over thirty-five was euthanized. "You won't have any complaints."

"Bring her by tomorrow night for a look-see. It'll be slow."

Meaning Roark wasn't going to make any promises unless he liked what he saw. "No problem."

After Roark left, Acevedo reclaimed his spot by the window. The young woman was still there. He signaled to one of his men on the floor to send her up to his office. If he couldn't have Zaria, he'd settle for her look-alike instead.

Chapter 15

Zaria wiped her mouth with her napkin, then tossed it onto her plate. Although she was hungry, she couldn't force herself to finish. They'd eaten during a silence that fell somewhere between uncomfortable and pure torture. Actually, Drew had wolfed his sandwich down in about two minutes. She was the one lingering.

"What's next on the agenda?" he asked.

"I'm going to take a shower." That was the first thing she'd wanted to do since walking in the door. She'd put it off, only because she didn't want Drew to guess how much being with Acevedo—she couldn't think of him as Jimmy anymore—had bothered her. She wanted to wash his touch from her skin, his smell from her body. "Will you be here when I get out?"

"I've got nowhere else to be."

A typical slick answer from him, but she did notice his perusal of her, as if checking to see if anything was wrong. "I won't be long."

Once inside the shower, she scrubbed every inch of her Acevedo had touched. Then she leaned her forehead against the cool tile and let the water rain down on her. Her thoughts went to Drew, whom she hoped was still sitting in the living room. She'd gotten just what she'd expected from Acevedo, but what had that Drew business been about? He'd popped into her mind and she hadn't questioned it. But why had he? It wasn't like she didn't have an adequate list of men she'd actually been with to conjure up.

It was an aberration, born of the fact that she knew he was listening. That's what she planned to keep telling herself. She had no intention of joining that flavor-of-the-moment club that he didn't even deny having. But she couldn't help acknowledging that the images in her head had been potent, turning her on enough to be able to fake the same with the man who held her.

Damn. She didn't need this now when the circumstances of the case would, if anything, bring them into closer company. If he'd told Acevedo that she belonged to him, she'd bet a time would come when he'd have to prove that one way or another—or appear to. Especially now that she was concerned for his safety. She wouldn't put it past Acevedo to try to get him out of the way in some way other than paying him off. It would be better if they watched each other's backs from now on, which meant it made more sense for Drew to stay here. She doubted Schraft would be willing to come up with another apartment. As dicey as this one was, it offered protection from anyone knowing her real address, which wouldn't be true for Drew if he went home.

Damn. Damn. Damn. She banged her forehead against the shower wall with each syllable.

A moment later she heard Drew's voice on the other side of the door. "Are you okay in there?"

"I'm fine," she called back. She snapped off the faucet. She'd been in there long enough. After toweling off, she changed into a pair of jeans and an oversize T-shirt and wrapped her hair in a towel. She'd deal with it later. For now she had to settle things with Drew.

He was back on the sofa when she came into the living room. The lunch dishes were gone. She didn't know if he'd washed them or simply removed them, but she didn't care. She took her usual spot on the sofa and pulled her legs up under her, nodding toward the bottle in his hand. The refrigerator had been stocked when they got there. She'd purchased a few items, including the

wine she'd offered him last night, from a store around the corner.
"I didn't know we had beer."

"It was in the back. Want one?"

She doubted Schraft had allowed someone to buy them
alcohol. It must be from the previous tenant, but beer didn't go
bad, did it? "Please."

When he returned from the kitchen she took the opened bottle
that he offered her and took a long drink. The cool liquid flowed
down her throat, warming her. "Thanks."

"Feeling better?"

"Was I that obvious?"

"No. I just know you, kid." He chucked her on the chin play-
fully. "You don't get quiet like that without a reason."

That was true, but she said anyway, "Maybe I was contemplating the best way to skewer you."

"The second time, maybe."

That's what she'd been referring to, but obviously he'd meant
the first. She hadn't given much thought to how she'd been then.
All she'd cared about was getting out of there.

"Still mad at me?"

She shook her head. She tended to heat up quickly and cool
down as fast. And in some ways she could see why he'd done what
he did, considering her crack about upchucking on the upholstery.
She hadn't been serious, but he must have thought she was. She
simply hadn't wanted to rehash it anymore. "Did I hurt you?"

For a second he gave her a look that said she had to be kidding.
Then his expression turned more sober. "There's one more thing."

"What's that?"

"I think I should stay here."

He thought she'd object? To tease him, she said, "I thought
you liked sleeping in your car."

He made a mock groan. "My spine still isn't speaking to me."
He made some more groaning noises as he got up. "I've got a
bag in the trunk."

Why was she not surprised? It wasn't until after he left that
she contemplated the logistics of their new arrangement. Neither
one of them was short enough to fit on the sofa and there was
only one bed. An image of the two of them there formed in her

mind, but it had nothing to do with sleep. She shook her head, as if doing so would shake that picture out of it.

Her cell phone rang and she rushed to retrieve it from the love seat where she'd left her purse.

"Hello, Zaria." Acevedo's voice came through the phone. "I'm not disturbing you, am I?"

Now he wanted to pretend he had manners. "No, of course not. I hope you have good news for me."

"Maybe. Have you heard of a club called Sinsations?"

She passed it on the highway every time she went into Manhattan. She didn't know anything about the clientele, but the place was huge. "Yeah."

"Meet me there tomorrow night at nine o'clock. I'll leave your name at the door."

"We'll be there."

She clicked off the phone before Acevedo had time to comment on the fact she planned to bring Drew along. After that afternoon, he had to assume that she would.

Drew nodded to the phone still in her hand. "Who was that?"

"Our friendly neighborhood pervert."

Drew set his bag down by the love seat. "He's got something already?"

"He wants to meet tomorrow night. Isn't that what we wanted?"

"Yeah, but damn."

That had been her first reaction, too. "Do you think we should tell our friends about the meeting?"

He grinned. "Maybe the boys could use a night out."

"Why do I have the feeling you're going to enjoy this way, way more than I am?"

"I haven't a clue."

Yeah, right. "I guess that means we have a reprieve for the moment, anyway."

Drew settled on the sofa beside her. "So what do you want to do now?"

Zaria yawned. "I'd settle for a good night's sleep for a change."

"So would I, but it's only four-thirty in the afternoon."

Zaria glanced at the clock above the TV. It was still early enough. "In that case, I'm going to visit my grandmother."

"Weren't you there yesterday?"

"Yes, but I went to ask her what she remembered about Acevedo. I think I upset her, then I left without giving her a decent explanation. Besides, today is my regular day to visit."

"Give me a minute to get ready, then I'll take you."

"There's no need. I'm not planning to stay that long." Just enough time to say hello to her grandmother and to ask the security staff to be extra vigilant over her grandmother for the time being. In retrospect, telling Acevedo her grandmother was at Pine Forest wasn't the brightest move. At the time, when she was still considering that he might be dug into this business too deep, it had seemed logical. If she came out here and if he was having her followed, he'd already know her connection to the place, preventing the need for too many questions.

In the second place, Acevedo might be able to claim that he and Zaria hadn't been that close, but he couldn't claim the same with her grandmother. Half the neighborhood had referred to Rosario Fuentes as *abuela* or *mami,* or some other appellation that indicated they regarded her as a grandmotherly figure. Acevedo had not been an exception. As long as Acevedo continued to buy her cover, she doubted Acevedo would do anything to harm her grandmother. Finally, the security staff at the facility was excellent.

"Where's your car?" Drew asked, pulling her from her thoughts.

Zaria pictured her car in her mind's eye, parked in the little lot next to her apartment, where it belonged. "Point taken," she said.

Drew rose from the sofa. "I won't be long."

She sank back against the sofa, propping her feet on the edge of the coffee table as he walked away, not as annoyed about the situation as she probably should be. Actually, it would be nice to have company on the trip for a change and the guarantee Drew wouldn't be skulking around the bushes waiting for her.

Chapter 16

Drew walked into the facility's dayroom a step behind Zaria. She'd been quiet the entire drive over. Her silence bothered him as it always did, but this time for purely selfish reasons—when she grew still like that, it was impossible to read her.

He still didn't know if she was ticked at him for surveilling the apartment or if her encounter with Acevedo still weighed on her. Even if the last possibility was the one that bothered her, he doubted having had Acevedo's hands on her was the problem. She'd expected that and, to Drew's mind, she probably could have prevented even that if she'd wanted to. He was certain it was the betrayal that got to her, since he knew she'd started out holding some hope that her childhood friend was innocent in this. Up until the excursion into the zoo, he'd heard her refer to him several times as Jimmy, and only as Acevedo once they'd come out.

Rosario Fuentes's eyes lit up the minute she recognized him walking in with her granddaughter. She stood to greet Zaria warmly, then turned to him.

She greeted him as she always did, as if he were one of her own. "*¿Como estas, papo?* It's about time you come to visit me."

He had to lean way down to accept her waiting embrace. He didn't bother to answer in the same language. Although he understood Spanish, he spoke it as well as an antelope navigated a hat shop. "It's good to see you."

She patted his arm. "Sit, sit. What's going on with the two of you? Do you need more information?"

"No, *Abuela*," Zaria said as she and her grandmother settled into the two chairs by the window. "We just came to visit."

Drew pulled a chair over and sat next to Zaria, draping his arm along the back of her chair.

Rosario patted his knee. "I'm glad my granddaughter is finally listening to me. I asked her to bring you by the last time she was here."

He cast a sideways look at Zaria. That's not how he'd heard it. "Really?"

Rosario rubbed her arms. "It is a little chilly in here today, though. My red sweater is on my bed."

She glanced pointedly at Zaria, obviously intending for her to get it. Almost as obvious was the fact that Zaria's grandmother wanted her out of the room for a few minutes. Zaria opened her mouth as if she'd protest, but in the end she stood and took the room key from her grandmother. "I'll be right back," she promised.

Drew turned to watch her departure, his attention focused on the sway of her hips as she walked away. When he turned back to Rosario it occurred to him he should have been more circumspect with his perusal. She looked back at him with a knowing smile.

He smiled back. "What did you want to speak to me about?"

Rosario sat back, folding her hands in her lap, her expression more serious than it had been before. "I know she's investigating something to do with a boy from our old neighborhood."

"Yes, Jaime Acevedo. What about him?"

"Is she being careful?"

How was he supposed to answer that? No less so than usual? That wouldn't be particularly helpful since Rosario believed as he did that her granddaughter was sometimes more reckless than she needed to be. "Grandma, you're asking me to tattle."

She shrugged. "Maybe. But I have a bad feeling about this. I know Zaria. She can be loyal to a fault. If she thinks this Jimmy is innocent..."

Her words trailed off and he understood her fear, that Zaria would leave herself vulnerable because she'd have a hard time believing her friend could be involved in anything illegal. He'd worried about that himself, but Zaria had already proven she was smarter than that. "That isn't a problem."

She scrutinized him a moment, probably wondering what had caused him to speak with such certainty. He thought she'd question him on that, but she smiled and patted his knee. "You know I count on you to watch out for her."

Way not to put too much pressure on him, but he already knew that. "I do my best." All she'd allow him to do. "She's a smart girl."

"Still, sometimes she doesn't see what's right in front of her."

He couldn't argue with that, either, but she fastened a look on him that appeared to communicate something he wasn't picking up on. He'd assumed at first that what Rosario sought from him was reassurance that her granddaughter wasn't putting herself in unnecessary danger. He wasn't so sure now. "What's your point?"

"These eyes may be old, *papo,* but they're not blind. I see how you look at her. If you plan to do something about that I wish you'd hurry up before she saddles me with one of those—how you say—buppies for a grandson."

Obviously Zaria had come by her directness honestly. He wouldn't hold his punches, either. "I'm not what she's looking for."

"What does she know? She thinks all there is to picking a man is how much money he has. And that's my fault. Growing up, I couldn't offer her much. She was always the one to provide for us. Her money paid for our first decent apartment, this place here." She gestured in a way that encompassed their surroundings. "I know she can barely afford it, but she wanted a place where she knew I'd be well cared for. I appreciate that, but I know what it costs her."

Drew doubted Rosario referred to cost purely in monetary terms. "She loves you."

"And that girl means more to me than I can ever tell you. I want to see her happy, but I don't think she will be if she keeps on her current course. That last one she brought to see me was the worst." She made a comical horrified face.

Drew chuckled. "You don't have to worry about him anymore."

"So I heard, but what's to prevent her from finding another one?"

Nothing, he supposed, except for the time being he wasn't letting her out of his sight. Come to think of it, she'd been gone longer than he felt comfortable with. How long did it take to retrieve one sweater? The only thing that kept him from going into full protective mode was the fact that when he glanced over his shoulder he saw her advancing toward them with a beige sweater in her hands.

Zaria stopped by her grandmother's chair to drape the sweater around her shoulders. "I couldn't find the red one. I hope this one's okay."

Rosario patted Zaria's hand, but her gaze was on him. "It's fine."

Drew shook his head but said nothing. He wouldn't have put it past Rosario to have deliberately asked for a sweater that wasn't there just to keep Zaria busy.

They stayed a little longer, until Rosario seemed to tire. On the way back to the highway, he stole a glance at Zaria. She hadn't said much since they got back to the car. "How are you doing over there?"

She sighed. "I'm fine. Why?"

"You haven't said two words to me since we started driving."

She shrugged. "I'm feeling a little melancholy, I guess. I know my grandmother needs to be here. They monitor her medically and besides, she's got friends here, a life. When I had her with me, about all she did was sit around wondering when I'd get home. But sometimes I really miss her."

"Is that the reason for the cat?"

"I told you he adopted me, not the other way around. I don't even like cats."

"If you say so." He glanced over at her again. She was still looking out the window with her elbow resting on the door frame and her head propped up on her hand. At least she was smiling now.

He checked the dashboard clock. They'd killed a couple of hours, but there was plenty of time left in the day. "Where to now?"

"Home, I guess, unless you have something you need to do."

Yeah, home—to Schraft's World of White. He didn't want to take her back there yet, not without an obvious means of passing the time. Even though Zaria's grandmother's words still rang in his ears, he had no intention on acting on them, at least not tonight. Lacking anywhere else to go, he had no choice.

"Home it is," he said, but he wasn't looking forward to it.

Traffic going over the Bridge was its usual Sunday-evening nightmare. All those folks who headed out to summer houses or to visit the relatives or whatever had to make it back to the city in time for work on Monday morning. Luckily, Drew and Zaria had stopped for gas along the Turnpike so that they weren't starving or in danger of having the car stop dead. But her stomach rumbled its disappointment at not being fed.

"Hungry?" Drew asked, as he maneuvered the car into the lane to catch the Cross Bronx.

"Very."

"How about a detour to City Island? I wouldn't mind some seafood."

Neither would she, especially on the Bronx's version of a fishing village. "Sounds like a plan."

A half hour later, Drew pulled into the parking lot of Neptune's, one of the newer restaurants that featured dining al fresco in the summer. For a Sunday night, the place was busy. Several groups were already seated in the bar waiting for tables.

"Do you want to wait or go somewhere else?" Drew asked her once the hostess informed them it would be twenty minutes before they would be seated.

Considering they'd have to pay the valet for parking either way it didn't make sense to go. "Let's stay. You can buy me a frozen margarita." She nodded toward the bar.

Drew took the beeper the hostess offered, hearing her decision. "How about a walk instead? We're right by the water."

"In case you hadn't noticed, this is October, not August."

"It's not that cold out."

No, it wasn't, but she could imagine the chilly breeze coming off the water. Still, she allowed him to lead her outside along the edge of the building to a small walkway at the back of the restaurant. Stopping at the railing, she looked out over the ocean. Several boats, mostly smaller craft, were moored close to the shore. Farther out on the horizon, the quarter moon cast silvery light on the dark water. Just as she'd imagined, the chilly breeze blew over her, stirring her hair around her face and making her shiver.

She looked up at Drew, who'd stopped beside her. "Okay, so it's a beautiful night."

Smiling, he brushed a strand of hair from her face. "Cold?"

"A little."

He took off his jacket and draped it around her shoulders. The leather was warm and soft and smelled of him. She inhaled.

"Better?" he asked.

She nodded, not trusting her voice at that moment. For a while, neither of them said anything, simply enjoyed watching the water lap up on the sand. Then she felt Drew shift. They were so close that their arms resting on the railing touched. She looked up at him to find him staring down at her. Despite the lack of light, she saw the warmth in his eyes as he regarded her, the smile on his lips that made his dimples appear.

How long had he been staring at her, and why did seeing the way he looked at her send a jolt of feminine awareness through her body? It had never surprised her that he had women practically falling into his bed, but she'd never expected to find herself so stirred up simply by standing next to him.

It was that damn fantasy she'd indulged in while Acevedo touched her. It had to be. Or that's what got her thinking out of whack. Even now, his expression seemed more one of concern than desire.

She looked away, out at the ocean, choosing what she hoped would be an innocuous avenue of conversation. "By the way, what did you and my grandmother talk about while I was gone?"

"The usual. She's worried about you."

"What is it this time? I'm working too hard or I'm not being careful enough?"

"Actually, I think she's more worried you'll hook up with another one of those—how you say—buppies she can't stand."

That sounded like her grandmother, especially the way Drew

said it. Although she greeted whomever Zaria brought around
with graciousness, Zaria knew her grandmother didn't approve
of her taste in men. After Harry, Zaria was beginning to agree
with her. All this time, she'd been looking for someone stable,
dependable, solid. Or at least that's what she'd been telling
herself. In reality she'd been looking for someone safe whom
she could control. Then when she found what she claimed she
wanted, she rejected it. What did that say about her?

"Well, if you've got any ideas, I'd love to hear them. I'm open
to suggestion at this point."

"You expect me to give you advice on who to go out with?"

"Why not? You haven't exactly been thrilled with who I've
dated, either. Here's your chance to put your two cents in."

He didn't say anything to that, but he turned to face her more
fully. His hand rose to stroke her hair back from her face. She
had to fight the urge to let her eyes drift shut so that she could
concentrate on the gentle touch of his fingers. Instead she held
his gaze that had suddenly grown more intense.

He exhaled, but still he said nothing. Maybe he wanted her
for himself, but didn't have the words to tell her. Yeah, that was
likely. She was only seeing now what she wanted to see, though
she wasn't sure why she wanted to see it. Besides, all she was
feeling was a tremendous case of lust, which she didn't need to
ruin her friendship with him to assuage. Nothing between them
could go anywhere, not as long as they worked together,
probably not even if they didn't.

But when the beeper in Drew's pocket went off, she pulled
away from him, feeling more than a little disappointed.

Drew pulled up in front of the apartment building and cut the
engine. He'd indulged in a couple of beers that had left him
feeling more melancholy than mellow. Neither of them had
finished much of their dinner, hence Zaria held a shopping bag
containing the remnants of both of their meals on her lap. He
couldn't say what her problem was, but he'd lost his appetite the
same moment he'd let the opportunity slip to tell her how he felt.
She'd looked up at him with those big brown eyes of hers and
for a moment he'd imagined that what she really wanted from

him was something other than dating tips. He'd wanted to tell her, but for once in his life his big mouth didn't seem to work.

Luckily, the hour was late enough that there was nothing left to the night except to go to sleep. If sleep came; that was the big *if*. He doubted he'd find slumber without at least a couple of hours of castigating himself for keeping silent.

Once he let them into the apartment, Zaria went to the kitchen to put away the leftovers. In the meantime, he went to the living room to find his bag. He'd change into his sweatpants and find some way to squeeze himself onto that short sofa, or if there were enough blankets he'd bunk on the floor.

He'd just found the sweatpants and slung them over his shoulder when he sensed her behind him. "About the sleeping arrangements," she said.

"What about them? I'll be out here. I'd appreciate a pillow if you can spare one."

She folded her arms. "If you tried to sleep on that thing you'd look like that Dr. Seuss character with his feet sticking out of the bottom of the bed."

No doubt, but that didn't change anything. "What's the alternative?"

"You could share the bed with me."

His groin tightened at the thought of it. "You're kidding, right?"

She tilted her head to one side and her gaze narrowed. "Sure. We could put a line of police tape down the center. No crossing over."

He didn't miss the sarcasm in her tone. He knew she wasn't serious but he felt the need to voice his objection. "I don't think so."

"Look, Grissom, stop being obtuse. You slept in that damn car last night, while I slept in a nice comfortable bed."

She expected him to find sleep in a bed that still held her scent. Yeah, that would happen. "That isn't necessary."

She threw up her hands. "Fine. I'm too tired to argue. I'll see you in the morning."

She walked past him. The temptation to stop her and tell her what he should have said earlier assailed him, but he let her pass.

That moment had slipped past him, perhaps forever. While that bothered him, he wasn't going to dwell on that now. Being here reminded him that they were together for a purpose—getting close enough to Acevedo to find out what he'd done with those girls. Until that was accomplished, they could both do with having a clear head.

He kept telling himself that, but on some level he wondered if he were simply being a coward, since he didn't know what he'd do if he came clean to her only to have her tell him she could never feel the same way. He didn't know what impact that would have on their friendship, but it couldn't be good. That's the prospect that kept his mouth shut and his libido in check—could he risk everything and end up with nothing instead?

The next morning Zaria roused herself at seven o'clock. She hadn't slept much and doubted spending any more time in bed would produce a better result. Her stomach rumbled from having been fed insufficiently the day before. She may as well get up and get her day, such as it was, started.

She'd slept in only an oversize T-shirt. She got out of bed and tugged on her sweatpants and headed for the bathroom. Surveying her image in the mirror, she stuck out her tongue. She looked like hell. Dark circles under her eyes attested to her lack of sleep. The salt air had turned her hair into a frizzy mess. She bound it at her nape with an elastic band, then washed her face and brushed her teeth.

She was a bit more presentable now, but what did it matter? She'd given Drew an in to let her know if he had any feelings for her last night and he hadn't taken it. If that weren't enough, the shocked look that had come over his face when she suggested they share the bed was proof the thought had never occurred to him, at least not seriously.

If anyone had told her a week ago that she'd give one good damn what Drew Grissom thought of her as a woman she'd have laughed herself silly. But she had to admit that it stung more than a little bit that he had no interest in her sexually. Not when she couldn't seem to get thoughts of him out of her head. He could sleep with half the women in the western world, but not her?

Mentally she shook her head. How stupid was this? She should be glad that nothing extraneous stood in the way of their friendship or their ability to work together. Now if she told herself that a few more times, maybe she'd believe it.

Chapter 17

Drew pulled up in front of the sign for the club's valet parking a little after nine. Looking up at the club's sign, he would have sworn, were it not for the cheesy name, that he'd mistakenly arrived at the Harvard Club. A discreet awning flanked by a pair of bronze lion plaques were the only adornment on the white exterior. He got out of the car and left the motor running then went around to collect Zaria, who was being helped from the car by another attendant.

She wore a two-piece black outfit that dipped low between her breasts and left most of her midriff bare. She wore her hair dead straight, a style he'd never seen on her, but one that flattered her. When he reached her, he pulled her closer with his hand at her bare waist. Unconsciously, his hand flexed. He could feel the muscle beneath his fingertips but her skin was incredibly soft.

Another man, one almost as big as he was, waited to open the door for them. "Welcome to Sinsations," he said. When Zaria gave him her name he signaled another man to come over to take them inside.

A doorway on the other side of the marble foyer led to a large, open room decorated in dark wood and a deep shade of pink. Large mirrors hung on the walls and decorated pillars around the room. Club chairs clustered around low tables took up most of the space, but there were maybe three poles throughout the room as well as a main stage flanked on either side by a bar and a DJ's booth. While not packed, there was a decent-size crowd for a Monday night. Waitresses in skimpy costumes and strippers dressed in even less circulated through the crowd. At every available post women gyrated to the cranked-up music.

As far as strip clubs went, this was class. Unless they were keeping Acevedo's women chained in the basement, he couldn't see this being the spot. He had the feeling this was another of Acevedo's tests, seeing how far he could trust Zaria, or maybe him. Whatever, they'd play what they were given and see where it took them.

They were led up a set of stairs at the other end of the club. There was a doorway on either side of them. To the left a modest sign read Champagne Suites, probably small rooms that afforded complete privacy. To the right was the VIP room.

The attendant held the door on the right open for them. "Please enjoy your time with us."

Drew let go of Zaria's waist to let her precede him into the room. Although much smaller than the room downstairs it was larger than Drew expected. The walls were painted the same dark pink as the chairs downstairs. A set of low, circular couches ringed the room. The far wall was made entirely of what must be reflective glass. From downstairs it had looked like a bank of mirrors.

Acevedo was already sitting on one of the couches to the right, a girl on either side of him. One had on a short black skirt; the other wore a light-colored thong. Neither wore anything above the waist. An interesting display, but what exactly was the point? Was he trying to show what a big man he was? The girls weren't free, unless they'd changed the rules at this sort of place and not told him. Then again, whoever owned this place was a friend of Acevedo's, or that's what he'd led them to believe. Comped at a strip club, now there was a concept. But from the way Acevedo's gaze was riveted on Zaria, he probably hoped to make her jealous.

"Come in," Acevedo said. "Roark will be here in a minute."

Drew took Zaria's hand and led her to sit across from Acevedo.

"So, Zaria," Acevedo continued. "What do you think of the place?"

"I've got nothing to complain about so far. They must make a killing to keep so much staff."

Acevedo shrugged. "I wouldn't know about that. Would you like some champagne?"

The girls had already set about pouring two glasses without being asked, so the question was moot. He accepted his from one of the girls and downed half its contents in one swallow. Not bad. Zaria had her legs crossed. When he sat back he put his hand on her thigh, more to annoy Acevedo than anything else. "Who did you say we were waiting for?"

Frowning, Acevedo's gaze went from where Drew's hand rested to his face. If looks could kill, Drew would be a dead man, but since they couldn't, he winked at Acevedo instead.

Acevedo tapped one girl's thigh. "Why don't you see if your boss is available."

While they waited, Drew focused on Zaria. They were so close together that he smelled her perfume, a soft, subtle fragrance he hadn't noticed before. Their eyes met, and he wondered if she was as stirred up as him at the moment. That had nothing to do with their surroundings, only her. He ran his hand down her thigh and back again to let it rest higher than it had been before. She shifted slightly, in a manner that might look like discomfort, but he didn't think so. Maybe she wasn't as immune to him as he thought.

A door opened on the opposite side of the room. Drew pulled his gaze from Zaria to see an older man, short, dark skinned with a pockmarked face, enter the room. With a nod of his head, he shooed the remaining girl from the room and sat next to Acevedo.

Acevedo straightened himself from his slouched position a little. "Roark, this is the young lady I told you about."

Zaria leaned forward, extending her hand. "Pleased to meet you. I'm Zaria Bennett."

Roark shook her hand. "Manners, I like that."

More than likely Roark liked the spectacular view of her cleavage she'd just given him.

Roark regarded him. "And you are?"

Drew extended his hand. "Jackson."

Roark dismissed him almost immediately, returning his attention to Zaria. "What do you think of the club?"

As Zaria answered, Drew focused on Acevedo. His gaze on Zaria was one of undisguised lust. Drew was tempted to offer him a napkin to wipe the drool off his chin. Drew had the satisfaction of knowing Acevedo would never have her, but one day he'd make sure to make the man pay for touching her at all.

Drew focused in again when Roark stood. "We'll be back in a moment." He held out a hand to Zaria, which she took.

Since he'd heard Roark mention something about showing her around, he didn't object. But in a minute, the two of them were gone, leaving him alone with Acevedo.

Chapter 18

Drew leaned back, draping his arms across the back of the sofa, waiting to see what would transpire. Almost immediately, the two girls returned, bringing a third girl with them. At first he thought Acevedo was just getting greedy until the last girl sat down next to him. This guy had to be kidding. Drew pulled a bill from his pocket and held it out for the girl to take. "Thanks, but no thanks. I prefer entertainment I don't have to pay for."

The girl looked at Acevedo for direction. He nodded toward the door. She took the bill from Drew's fingertips, stuffed it in her G-string and left.

Acevedo shrugged. "It's your loss." He made a show of fondling one girl's breasts. "But I prefer entertainment that doesn't steal my money and cut out of town."

Drew laughed. "And what? You don't think she'll do the same to you and your little friend, too? Zaria is out for Zaria. She doesn't give a damn about you."

Acevedo's face colored, letting Drew know he'd hit his mark. He'd checked the man out, read the newspaper accounts. Most men in Acevedo's position would be content to make their money, in legal ways or not, and leave it at that. They didn't seek out the spotlight or require adoration from those around them. In his heart, Acevedo was still that insecure kid from the hood who wanted everyone to love him.

Before he could manage a comeback, his cell phone rang. One of the girls fished it out of his jacket pocket and handed it to him. Did they jump through flaming hoops, too?

Acevedo answered the call, not saying much, but seeming to grow more agitated the longer whoever was on the phone talked. "Excuse me," he said finally and took himself and his phone out the door.

Drew would love to know what that was about, but the minute Acevedo was out the door, the girls turned their attention to him. "Uh, no." He nodded toward the side door. "Come back when your friend does."

As they left, Zaria came in. She glanced at Acevedo's empty side of the couch, but came directly to him, surprising him by snuggling next to him with her legs folded beneath her and her hand on his chest. She leaned up to whisper in his ear. "This room is monitored."

He'd figured as much, though he hadn't detected a camera. But he knew what she was telling him. Nobody watching would buy them sitting there twiddling their thumbs waiting for Acevedo to get back.

He tangled his fingers in her hair, drawing her head back so he could see her face. She looked at him with a sloe-eyed siren's smile that did something wicked to the pit of his stomach. Was that genuine or part of the act? There was only one way to find out and he was willing to risk another shot to the gut to know. He lowered his head and claimed her mouth.

Her lips parted beneath his and her tongue sought his. He didn't hold back from her. His arms closed around her, bringing her to her knees, as his tongue plunged into her mouth. She responded by sliding one of her legs between his to straddle him. His fingers gripped her hips, grounding him during that wild, wild kiss.

Eventually, she pulled away to lean against him and whisper, "I think that should do it."

He blinked as her words sank in. So it had been for show. If she'd laid one like that on Acevedo, no wonder he was champing at the bit. Well, he had his answer, anyway. But if she expected him to get up and walk out after that, she'd be disappointed. "Give me a minute, okay?"

She smiled at him in a way he couldn't begin to comprehend and pulled away. She sat next to him and refilled her champagne glass, taking a dainty sip. She glanced up at him. "Do you want some?"

He shook his head. He didn't want to share one more thing Acevedo had had first. But thinking about her with him had killed his libido. "Let's get out of here." He walked to the door and held it open for her. She put down the glass and followed.

Once in the car, Zaria put her hands in her hair and shook. "What's the matter?"

Those were the first words Drew had spoken to her since he'd said he wanted to go. "Nothing much. I just feel like I want to get that place off of me. It's like the Bizarro World in there."

"How so?"

"This guy, Roark, acts like he's running the Plaza, when all it is is a strip club. Oh, excuse me, the premiere gentlemen's club in the Bronx. He seems to be aboveboard—no drugs, no touching, at least on the main floor. Upstairs is different. In the room we were in, you can get a little friskier. That's why he claims he has the room monitored, to protect the girls. In the private rooms, who knows? Roark doesn't monitor them, but the official policy is no happy endings. If you ask me, we're wasting our time with him."

When Drew said nothing to that, she studied his profile as best she could in the dark interior of the car. He was looking straight ahead, paying her no attention, his jaw tight. Unless she'd missed something, what was that about? "What happened to Acevedo?"

"He got a phone call and left."

If Drew knew what that call was about, he'd have told her, so that couldn't be what bothered him. Zaria stared out the window. Due to the lack of traffic, they were almost back at the apartment. She'd let it rest until they got there.

When they got back to the apartment, Zaria went to the sofa to slip off her shoes. Drew still hadn't said one word to her that wasn't necessary. He took off his jacket and slung it over the love seat. Afterward, he stood there like he was waiting for some-thing.

"What?"

"You're on my bed."

She cocked her head to one side and considered him. He couldn't honestly be contemplating sleeping here. She'd resigned herself to that earlier. At least she wouldn't hang off the end by at least a foot.

But that wasn't what concerned her now. "What exactly is the matter with you?"

"Who says anything's the matter?"

"I do." She would have chucked him on the chin as he'd done to her earlier if he'd been close enough. "I know you, kid, and you don't get this quiet, period." He shot her a droll look, letting her know her humor had once again fallen flat. Then a thought occurred to her. "Was it the club? Was it too much?"

"That's quite a talent you have there. No wonder you've got Acevedo panting after you."

Zaria ground her teeth together. That's what this was about? He thought she'd used him in the same way she had Acevedo. In a way she had. She'd cozied up to him to make an impres-sion, but when he'd kissed her she'd wanted it. And despite where they were, she'd gotten a little carried away. Did he hold it against her that she'd managed to make him respond the same way?

Drew's gaze hardened. "What did you let him do to you?"

She wondered when he'd get to asking her that and perhaps judging her for it. She had no intention of answering him. She'd done what she had to, no more, no less. "Isn't it a bit late for that?"

"Maybe. Tell me."

"Why? So you can hold it against me?"

"Why would I do that?"

"I don't know. You tell me."

He huffed out a breath. "Then answer me this. How is what you did with him any different than what you did with me?"

"I really don't know, Drew." She was tempted to tell him to

go to hell, but her natural honesty won out. "But I can tell you what they had in common. Both times I was thinking about you."

She'd had enough of this conversation. She rose from the sofa, intending to go to the bedroom. Let him sleep out here if that's what he wanted. Damn him.

She made it as far as the hallway before he caught up with her, grasping her forearm to bring her around to face him. "What do you mean, you were thinking about me?"

Did she have to spell it out for him? That something about this case, about him, had been getting to her? Too bad. She couldn't think of a coherent way to explain it. All she could manage was a baleful, "Drew…"

For a moment he didn't say anything, but the heat in his gaze was enough. He wanted her, and God help her, she wanted him, too. Her eyes drifted shut as his mouth claimed hers. His tongue met hers, and if anything the kiss was hotter than the last time. Her fingers went to the buttons on his shirt, then pulled the shirt-tails from his waistband. Parting his shirt, she pushed it from his shoulders. He shrugged out of it the rest of the way, letting it fall to the floor. She ran her fingers over his chest. She'd always assumed he was just a big guy, beefy not buff, but every inch of him underneath her fingertips was muscle.

"Oh God," she murmured, as his lips touched the side of her throat and his fingers tugged at the zipper to her top. Her breathing was shallow and her pulse accelerated. She inhaled, breathing in the scent of their mutual arousal.

She hadn't expected this—this heat, this combustibility between them. It was heady, overpowering. When he freed her and covered her bare breast with his palm, she moaned his name.

He lifted his head and his hand stilled. He didn't speak but she saw the questions in his eyes. Did she want him to stop? It didn't make sense any kind of way she looked at it; all that mattered to her was this moment. She leaned up and pressed her mouth to his. He groaned and lifted her, carrying her toward the bedroom.

He set her down beside the bed in the darkened room. The only light filtering in came from the quarter moon hanging low in the sky. They shed the last of their clothes before he pulled her down onto the bed on top of him. Their mouths met and his hands gripped her buttocks. She moaned into his mouth and her fingertips dug into his shoulders.

He pressed her onto her back and came over her, covering her with his body. She loved the feel of his weight on her, the way her body cradled his, the feel of his erection pressing against her. Her legs moved restlessly against his. It wasn't enough. She wanted him inside her. "Drew," she called to him.

He sheathed himself and thrust into her. Her back arched and she wrapped her legs around him, taking him deeper. He groaned against her throat, one hand grasping her hips as he moved inside her. She opened her eyes and looked up at him. She could barely make out his features in the darkness, but she heard his breathing, as rapid and shallow as her own.

Then his head lowered to her breast, first to circle its peak with his tongue, then to draw her nipple into his mouth. He thrust into her again and she lost it, her hips rocking against his as her orgasm claimed her. He pumped into her just as furiously, groaning his release against her throat.

For a long time, they lay together, recovering. Finally he raised himself on his elbows and looked down at her, stroking her hair from her face. "Baby, are you okay?" he asked.

She huffed out a breath. "Oh God, Drew, what did we just do?"

Chapter 19

Hearing Zaria's words, Drew froze. He didn't hear regret in her voice, but what she said suggested it. He'd asked her, though not in words, if she wanted to stop. Maybe he should have verbalized that thought, because the last thing he wanted her to feel was that by being with him she'd made a mistake.

He leaned over her to turn on the bedside lamp. She made a sound of protest and shaded her eyes. "Is that really necessary?"

He wanted to see her face, and that was the only way to accomplish it. "In answer to your previous question," he said, "I think it's called sex."

She lowered her hand and looked up at him. "No, I think you call it something else that begins with the letter *F*."

True, and when he'd imagined being with her, he hadn't imagined such a rough-and-ready affair, either. "Does that bother you?"

She shook her head, displacing her hair. "Not my usual style, I guess."

He could see that, considering the men she typically dated. He doubted even one of them could handle the passion he'd just seen in her. He'd barely survived it. The orgasm she'd brought him to had been one of the most explosive in his life. Simply thinking about it brought him fully erect again.

She sighed, a contented sound. "Maybe we should get some sleep."

Maybe. She did look exhausted, which wasn't doing his male ego any harm. But they hadn't settled anything between them. For all he knew, she considered this a one-night thing borne of them both getting a bit too stirred up.

He got up to dispose of the condom. When he returned, she rolled over and laid her head on his shoulder. That had to count for something. Their talk could wait until morning. But when he woke in the morning, her side of the bed was empty.

Zaria woke that morning to the sound of Drew's cell phone ringing. She got it out of his pants pocket, intending to hand it to him, but recognizing the number on the display she decided to answer it herself. "Good morning, Agent Gonzales," she said as a greeting. At least she thought it was still morning. She checked the display on the bedside clock. It read 7:34.

"Oh, Officer Fuentes. I thought I'd called Officer Grissom."

"You did. What can I do for you?"

"We've got some news. We're coming over."

Zaria ground her teeth together. "You do realize we could still be being watched."

"That won't be a problem."

Zaria wondered what he meant by that, but the phone line went dead before she had a chance to ask.

She looked over at Drew, who was dead to the world. She smiled, liking the idea of having worn him out with that one raw, sweaty encounter. She should have her brain examined for that. She didn't usually act so precipitously. She knew what kind of man he was. What they'd shared amounted to his usual entertainment any night of the week—no biggie, even if it was with her.

Well, she wasn't going to complain about it now. She hadn't realized it before, but she'd needed that release he'd given her. And what a release it had been. She should have known from the magic way his hands had massaged her feet that he'd be able to work a little magic everywhere else. At least she didn't have to worry about him wanting more from her. That could be disastrous for both of them. But she didn't regret her one night of recklessness. If anything, she wished there could be more.

She threw off the covers, found underwear, jeans and a T-shirt and headed for the bathroom. Gonzales hadn't said how quickly they were coming or from how far away they were. She couldn't greet them in the state she was in now. When she got herself presentable, she'd wake Drew.

As she came out of the bathroom, the doorbell rang. So much for waking up Drew. Both Gonzales and Spenser wore grim faces when she opened the door to them. "Where's Officer Grissom?" Spenser asked.

"He should be around in a minute," she said, not knowing if that was true or not. "Why don't we go in the kitchen. I'll make some coffee."

The two men seated themselves at the small table, while she went to the coffeemaker. "What gets you two up and out so early in the morning?"

"We found the other girls."

That came from Spenser. If they'd been found, why did he sound so glum? "Where?"

"One of the neighbors we hadn't interviewed before told the detectives she'd noticed them repaving the driveway a day before the fire. We finished digging it up last night. The girls were buried there."

Zaria bit her lip to keep the emotion from showing on her face. "How many were there?"

"Six."

Zaria turned away from them and squeezed her eyes shut. He'd killed them all. She could understand Acevedo ridding himself of a wayward girl and an ineffectual madam. The agent being killed was expected. But killing the other girls was an act of viciousness and vindictiveness, nothing more.

When she opened her eyes, Drew was standing there. Part of the reason she'd taken the men into the kitchen was so they couldn't see Drew emerge from the bedroom, in whatever state that might be. He'd obviously showered and shaved, though she hadn't heard him doing either.

"What happened?" he asked.

She looked up at him and saw the concern in his eyes. She stared back at him in a way she hoped asked him not to say or do anything to tip off the two men as to what they'd been doing last night. "They're gone, Drew. Acevedo killed them all."

He muttered a curse under his breath. He moved past her to get a mug and fill it with coffee. "Where does that leave us?"

"We won't be needing the two of you anymore. We'll get someone else on the inside, try to link Acevedo with ownership of the property."

Zaria looked from Gonzales to Spenser. Neither face told her anything. "Why would you do that? You already have us inside."

Gonzales said, "For one thing, your sergeant needs you back."

She could imagine there wasn't much of a team without the two of them, but that could wait. And they were ignoring something else. "Don't you think he'll try to replace them? If the business is as lucrative as you say it is, why should he give that up? He'll set up shop somewhere else and you'll be in the same spot you are now."

"But probably not for a while. He's too hot now."

Zaria huffed out a breath, then glanced at Drew, who stood with his arms folded, the mug in one hand. Of the three men, his expression told her the least. He couldn't be thinking of letting this go, not when they hadn't played it through. Who knew what they'd discover if they kept Acevedo on a string?

The men stood. Spenser said, "We thank you both for your efforts. We've let your sergeant know we won't be needing you after today."

Zaria stayed in the kitchen while Drew let them out. She slumped into one of the kitchen chairs, propped her elbows on the table and put her hands in her hair. Were they supposed to let it end like this, while he was still out there free to do what he wanted?

She lifted her head when Drew came back into the kitchen. His expression hadn't softened any, but he did say, "I'm sorry, baby."

She shook her head. "We can still get him."

"You heard what the man said. It's over."

"No. It's not. And I can't believe you of all people are willing to cave so easily. You, who does whatever he wants whenever he wants."

"Within reason. Is your ambition so important to you that you're willing to go after this guy with no authorization, no backup and no plan?"

Did he honestly think that's what this was about for her? "I'm not even thinking about that. He's dangerous and he's out there."

"And the Feds or whoever will have to get him. Give it up, Zaria."

She nodded, only to appease him. But she knew she wouldn't give up until Acevedo was put behind bars for a long, long time.

Chapter 20

Zaria looked out the back passenger window of the taxi that had brought her to Acevedo's social club. They'd cleared out of Schraft's world of white that afternoon. Once Drew left her at her apartment, she'd changed into another of the outfits she'd bought for her undercover wardrobe, thrown on her fur jacket and headed here. She thought she knew how to force Acevedo's hand and was determined to try it before she allowed herself to let go.

She paid the driver and got out of the car. She hadn't expected much to be going on inside on a weekday afternoon, but the place was full of kids of varying ages. They'd never had anything like this when she was growing up in the neighborhood, which was why everyone had congregated in the streets, getting themselves in trouble. It should be incongruous that a man who could do so much good could also do so much evil, but it was often the case. One activity provided cover for the other.

She found the doorway leading up to Acevedo's office. As usual a man stood by the door. "Can you let Mr. Acevedo know that Zaria Bennett is here to see him?"

He dislodged a small walkie-talkie from his belt. "There's a Zaria Bennett to see Mr. Acevedo." A moment later came the answer. "Mr. Acevedo said to send her up."

Mentally, Zaria shook her head. All this security for a man

who was supposedly aboveboard. She wondered why no one questioned this. Maybe they were too grateful for a place for their kids to play basketball in the afternoons to care.

Zaria passed through the door the man held for her and headed up the stairs. As she went up another man came down. She hoped that meant they would be alone.

He was sitting on the sofa when she reached the office. A pleased smile spread across his face when he saw her. "Where's your friend? I thought he didn't let you out of his sight."

Rather than join him on the sofa, she sat on the coffee table facing him and propped her feet on the sofa beside him. "Everybody's got to sleep sometime."

He chuckled. "What can I do for you, Zaria?"

She placed her hands on the coffee table and leaned back. "I came to tell you nice try, but no cigar."

His brow furrowed. "I thought Roark offered you the job."

"He did. I told him I'd have to think about it. I didn't want to refuse him while you were still there, but I'm not interested."

He put his hand on her booted calf and squeezed the muscle there. "Why not?"

"Your friend Roark is so freaking clean he squeaks when he walks. You and I both know I could work there a hundred years and never be able to get Jackson off my back." She lifted her leg to place the toe of her boot against his crotch. She was probably flashing him too, but she didn't care. "You do want to help me, don't you, Jimmy? Tell me you didn't see us together last night. He had his hands all over me. Did you like watching that?"

"No."

Liar. She saw it in the way his eyes narrowed and the way his hands rose to press her foot more firmly against his groin. He'd enjoyed watching. He'd enjoy doing even more. That's what she counted on. "Can't you get me something else?"

She pressed down on him and he groaned. Freaking pervert. She hoped he'd hurry up and answer her before he spent himself, since she didn't plan on giving him satisfaction of any kind.

"I might have something. In a few days."

"What? I can handle anything you want to give me."

"I bet you can."

She pulled her foot from his grasp and stood. "Do it soon, Jimmy. I like to finish what I start."

She walked out, hurrying down the stairs and out of the building. She hailed a passing livery cab and got in. In case anyone was watching her, she told the driver to take her to a mall in the Northeast Bronx. She'd kill some time in the Barnes & Noble there and then catch another cab home.

She kept an eye on the back window. Almost as soon as the cab drove off, a white van pulled away from the curb and pulled up behind them. The windows were tinted too dark for her to see the driver, but she'd bet one of Acevedo's goons was behind the wheel.

As long as he was content to follow, Zaria couldn't care less. Instead of Barnes & Noble bookstore, she'd head to the J.C. Penney department store. While whoever it was was watching one exit, she'd slip out the other.

She didn't get that far, though. At the next light the van swerved in front of the cab, blocking it in. She had her weapon in her hand in the next second. But it was Drew who got out of the van. He stalked over to her side of the car and yanked the door open. "Get in the van," he said.

Since she'd never seen such a look of fury on his face before, she wasn't going to argue with him. She got out as Drew tossed a bill to the driver. He slammed the door behind her then followed her to the van. He got in a second after she did, pulling the door closed with such force that the van shook. As the light had already changed and drivers behind them were already honking, he drove off.

She focused on fastening her seat belt and wondering how he'd found her. No one had followed her there. She'd checked. Despite the granite set of his jaw, she was going to ask him. "How did you know where to find me?"

He cast her a look that said she had to be kidding. "I know you, Zaria. I figured you'd show up there sooner or later, so I waited."

So, she'd been more transparent than she'd thought. "You don't have to get so bent out of shape. I wasn't in any danger."

"I know."

She shot him a questioning glance.

"You forgot the cell phone I gave you in your pocket."

She fished it out of her pocket and set it on the dashboard. "Where are we going?"

"To my house."

She didn't bother to ask why. He probably had a bed he wanted to chain her to in order to keep her out of trouble. She didn't remind him, either, that he could have known exactly what she was up to if he'd agreed to help her in the first place. For now she needed for him to listen to her.

"Before we do that, I want to check out an address. Acevedo had a bunch of papers and stuff on his table. This one jumped out at me since it's in Queens, not the Bronx."

"Later."

Zaria sighed and stared out the window. She supposed that curt answer was the best she was going to get out of him at the moment.

Drew's place was a two-story detached number just over the Westchester border. Zaria had been there a couple of times and already decided the house suited him. Most of the walls were painted a light beige, but the dark wood and heavy leather furniture seemed to fit.

He let her in the front door, then closed it behind them. The bag she'd rifled through to find her outfit but never unpacked sat in the hallway. Obviously, ringing her doorbell was just a formality for him.

"Are you hungry?" he asked.

Since the last time she'd eaten had been the afternoon of the day before, her stomach growled a resounding "yes." She followed him toward the kitchen. "What have you got?"

"How does steak sound?"

"Fine. Do you want me to help with anything?"

"How are you with salads?"

"I do all right."

He went to the refrigerator and tossed her a bag of prepared Caesar salad. "See what you can do with that."

She chuckled, relieved that his anger with her seemed to

have ebbed. She wanted his cooperation, not his ire. She found a salad bowl and utensils in the cabinet he indicated and tore open the bag of salad. Within fifteen minutes, they were seated at the kitchen table, enjoying a meal of steak, wild rice and the salad, but there hadn't been much conversation since they started preparing the food.

"So, Drew," she began, in an effort to lighten the mood. "Was there anything Freudian about your choice of *Jackson* as a cover?"

He shrugged. "It's a nice, strong name. Could be either first name or last name."

"It's your cousin's name."

"I was always jealous of that. What kind of name is Drew? That's something you already did on a piece of paper."

"I thought your given name was Andrew."

"It is. It was, until the first day of kindergarten. The teacher read a story, *Nobody Listens to Andrew,* about a kid named Andrew who sees a bear in the house but no one believes him. In the middle of the story, one of the other kids gets up, points at me and says, 'Maybe he just saw himself in the mirror.' I was not exactly a tiny kid. I've been Drew ever since."

Zaria sipped from her wineglass. She wouldn't put it past him to have made that whole story up, but it struck her as genuine. While he was being so agreeable, she'd ask him something else he'd never answered to her satisfaction. "Why did you turn down the bump to the detective squad?"

"I didn't want it." He forked a piece of steak into his mouth and chewed. "Maybe if the real world worked like it does on TV, that would be different. But I couldn't imagine myself chained to a desk, putting on a suit every day, talking nice to some punk rather than cracking him in the head. I'd bore myself silly. It's true the guys on the street are usually the ones who get the questions like, 'Why'd you have to shoot that poor guy fifty times?' but that's where I want to be."

She took another sip. Things weren't exactly as he told them, either. The days of cracking folks in the head were over for practically everyone, but she understood what he meant. He'd rather be there on the front line than the clean-up committee.

"Why do you want to be a detective so badly?"

She figured he'd get to that next. "A girl in my old neighborhood was raped by her boyfriend. The detectives didn't think it was worth going after, even though there had been a host of witnesses. How was she supposed to go on living there knowing her attacker was there, too, free to do it again if he wanted to? She killed herself."

"Were you one of them, witnesses I mean?"

She nodded. "For part of it." She sighed. "Those detectives let her down. I've always thought I could do better."

For a moment, neither of them said anything. They'd both eaten as much as they were going to. Drew said, "Why don't you go get changed and we'll check out this address of yours. If it looks like something, we'll try to get Gonzales and Spenser back on it. If not, we'll leave it alone. Deal?"

"Deal." She supposed she could live with that.

Chapter 21

Drew halted the van across the street from the address Zaria had given him. The storefront was unmarked and the windows papered over. Either something had just closed here or was about to open. From that distance it wasn't clear which.

There were only three stores clustered here, but it was evident this must be a Spanish-speaking neighborhood. The store on the corner was a bodega. Next to that was a *botanica*, a place to buy herbs, oils, candles and the like. The third was the location in question.

He glanced over at Zaria. "What do you think?"

"I think I need to go shopping."

He made a U-turn and pulled up in front of the shop. "Don't be too long."

"I won't."

He watched Zaria slide out of the van, shutting the door behind her. She disappeared inside the store. Telling her to stay where he could see her wouldn't have helped since the windows were made of glass tinted dark enough to write the store's specials on them in pink and white lettering. He had no idea what half the stuff on there was since it was written in Spanish. Part of him dreaded what she might come out of there with.

He shook his head, considering her. Damn, he admired her fearlessness, though it drove him crazy, too. Especially when it came to Acevedo. She'd walked back into his office, even though they now suspected him of killing six women simply to cover his tracks. Acevedo probably wouldn't have done anything to her with all those kids in the building, but he doubted she'd known beforehand that they'd be there. Hearing that story from her past, he thought he understood her better. She must have been a kid then, since he knew she'd moved from the neighborhood as soon as she'd graduated high school.

One more thing he knew was that if she ever put a hand, finger, thumb or toe on Acevedo again, he'd throttle her himself. How much of that did she think he could stand? Then again, she probably had no idea how much the previous night meant to him. She hadn't even mentioned it. The only indication she'd given him that she remembered being with him was the look she'd given him when he first came into the kitchen that morning. She'd been horrified at the thought of exposure, even to these men whom they barely knew and who held no sway on their futures. Judging by the looks the two men had given him as they left, neither had been fooled.

Zaria came out carrying a white plastic shopping bag. When she slid in beside him, he asked, "What did you get?"

"A couple of candles." She set the bag down at her feet and fastened her seat belt. "I spoke to the owner, *una bruja,* or so she claims. She says it's supposed to be some kind of health spa opening next door, but she hasn't seen any health equipment go in. She said she already worked *un trabajo* on the place."

Drew almost laughed. Now they had witches casting spells to add to their case. He refrained, only because he had no idea how superstitious Zaria was. She'd already worked enough *trabajos* on him. "Anything else?"

"The bodega next door is a front for selling drugs. She hasn't ratted them out since they sell her marijuana cheap."

This time Drew did laugh. "Let's get home." If he wasn't mistaken, somebody would want to watch this place, if not Gonzales and Spenser, then someone from the NYPD.

He pulled away from the curb, but he couldn't resist one gibe. "Was she a good witch or a bad witch?"

"I'll have to let you know later."

Now what the hell did that mean?

* * *

Spenser and Gonzales arrived at Drew's house together, neither of them looking pleased. "I thought we decided to put this to bed," Gonzales said once they were all seated in Drew's living room.

"I thought I could get something more from him." She'd stressed the word *I* since she'd only dragged Drew into this to protect her.

"And did you?"

"Two things. I told him the job at the club was too tame. He said he might have something more interesting in a couple of days."

"Is this on tape?"

She started to say no when Drew pulled a microcassette from his pocket and tossed it to Spenser. She should have known. Why bother to listen if he wasn't recording? She hadn't thought about that, though.

"Is there anything else?" Spenser asked.

"When I was in his office, I noticed a paper with this address on it." She pulled the slip of paper from her back pocket on which she'd written the address. "It's a storefront business in a Spanish neighborhood in Queens. The woman who owns the place next door doubts it's legit."

Spenser nodded. "Let us know if Acevedo contacts you again. Right away next time. In the meantime, we'll keep an eye on the place."

"If anything goes down, we want in."

Spenser nodded again. "Thanks." A few minutes later, the two men left, leaving her alone with Drew.

After closing the door behind the two men, Drew returned to Zaria. She was sitting on the sofa, her head back, her eyes closed, her feet propped on his coffee table. She looked as beat as he felt. He sat next to her, his body turned toward her, one elbow propped on the back of the sofa, his head resting on his palm.

He gave a strand of her hair a tug. "How are you doing over there?"

She gazed at him with sleepy eyes. "I'm fine."

Yeah, right. Zaria was putting up a tough front for him once again, but he wasn't buying it. He'd let her get some sleep eventually, but first there were a couple of things he needed to say. He gave that strand of hair another tug. "You did good today, baby."

"We did."

He shook his head. "That was all you, and you know it. I'm sorry. I should have backed you in the first place."

"Yeah, you should have."

He chuckled. "You don't pull any punches, do you?"

"Not if I can help it. Not for nothing, why didn't you?"

Drew swallowed. It was time to fess up, to admit his feelings for her. He dreaded it as much as he wanted to get it over with. For all he knew she'd laugh in his face or for whatever reason shoot him down. But it was a chance he had to take.

"I didn't want you anywhere near that guy. You have no idea how crazy it made me hearing you with him."

She studied his face with narrowed eyes. "Because of last night?"

He shook his head. "No." Beyond that, words failed him. He knew he should tell her he'd been falling in love with her for some time. She deserved that much honesty from him. But he couldn't find the words to say what he wanted.

But she must have picked up on it anyway. She looked away from him to where her hands rested in her lap. "I don't know what to say to you, Drew."

He sighed. At least there was no outright laughter. "You don't have to say anything."

She focused on his face, offering him a little half smile. "Why didn't you tell me?"

"I wanted to avoid an awkward conversation like the one we're having."

She shook her head. "Honestly, Drew, I don't know what I'm feeling, whether it's this case or you or the two of us so close together. All I know is that I needed last night. I needed you. I can't make you any promises, but I don't want to give that up until I have to."

Drew wondered what she meant by "having" to give it up,

but she reached up and pressed her mouth to his. Her tongue thrust into his mouth, seeking his. He sucked on it, drawing one of those moans he loved from her lips. His arms closed around her, pulling her across him onto his lap. He cradled her back with one arm. His other hand slipped beneath her shirt to rove upward, over her belly, her rib cage, to settle on her breast. He molded the soft flesh in his palm as his thumb stroked her nipple. Her back arched and her leg rose to rub against his side. Her fingers gripped his shoulder, urging him on.

He broke the kiss to pull her shirt over her head. He hadn't been able to see her last night, but now his gaze traveled over her. He strummed his thumb over one dark nipple before drawing her closer and taking it into his mouth. Her neck arched and she moaned his name.

He lifted his head and regarded her. His eyes burned and his breathing labored. "I'm here, baby," he whispered.

She smiled, her eyes half closed. Her fingers tugged at his shirt until he was free of it. He pulled her against him, loving the feel of her soft skin against his, and buried his face against her neck. He wanted to take it slower tonight, really please her, but she wasn't making it easy for him. Her hands went to the waistband of his jeans to unsnap them. She had him out of them in another minute, then stood to divest her own.

He pushed the coffee table away with one foot then backed her up enough so that he could sit in front of her. Grasping her hips, he brought her to his mouth. She cried out and clung to him, her fingers clasping his head to hold him to her. His tongue roved over her, delved inside her, lapping at the sweet juices flowing there.

Felt the tremors in her legs and knew she was close. She called his name, but he didn't stop. He drew her clitoris into his mouth and sucked hard until she cried out and her body spasmed. Only when she started to quiet did he pull her down to straddle him. She buried her face against his neck, her body still trembling. For the moment, she was sated, but his body was still rock hard and throbbing.

He put his hand in her hair and drew her head back. She gazed down at him with an impish smile on her face. He knew why a second later. He drew in his breath as her hand closed around him, squeezing his shaft. He shut his eyes, leaning back against the sofa, letting the pleasure of her touch wash over him. She leaned over slightly and he heard the sound of clothes rustling. He knew what she was doing and waited.

Only once she started to roll the condom on him did he open his eyes. With one hand he brought her mouth down to his. He used the other to lift her so that the tip of his erection rested at the entry to her body. He let her down slowly and they both shivered as her body enveloped him.

Then she started moving over him, slowly at first, then with increasing rapidity. His fingers dug into the flesh of her backside. He tried to hold back, wanting to take her with him, but he was almost there already. He slid his hand between their two bodies to stroke her. Almost immediately her back arched and she cried out his name against his lips. He buried his face against her throat and let his own orgasm overtake him, a powerful explosion that set his own body trembling.

He crushed her to him, his fingers gripping her back as he tried to breathe properly. He was a goner. He understood that now. He'd been kidding himself with this "falling" for her business. He was already down on the ground, looking up, wondering what happened to him.

He hadn't held anything back from her; he hadn't wanted to. He doubted he would have been able to if he tried. She took everything from him and gave him everything in return. He hoped to hell that meant she felt something for him, other than friendship and a phenomenal case of lust. If it didn't, he didn't know what he was going to do, but he'd have to figure it out later, as she started to stir.

She drew back and looked down at him, smiling. Her eyes scanned his face. "What are you thinking?"

He didn't dare tell her, not when he knew she hadn't made up her mind about him yet. He didn't want to push her, or worse, drive her away by confessing feelings he knew she didn't share. He smiled as best he could under the circumstances. "It's a good thing I had this carpet cleaned last week."

Chapter 22

Later, after they made it upstairs to Drew's big bed, Zaria lay with her head against his chest. As he'd pulled the covers over them, Drew had suggested they get some sleep, but neither of them had been able to find it. She never would, if his hands kept moving over her in the same lazy, erotic way. Whether he'd planned to or not, he'd managed to stir her up all over again.

She turned her head and kissed his chest, just above his nipple. She smiled when he jerked in response. Apparently he was in the mood to dish it out, but not to take it.

His hand stroked over her hair. "What are you doing?"

She circled her tongue around one nipple while her fingers strummed over the other. "You know damn well what I'm doing."

"I thought we were going to sleep."

That's what he said, but she could hear the humor in his voice, and the eagerness. "There's been a change in plans." She leaned up and pressed her mouth to his. He rewarded her by welcoming her tongue into his mouth for a slow, erotic kiss. One of his hands cradled her head; the other splayed low on her back, but drifted lower.

She moaned as his fingers grasped her buttocks, bringing her in greater contact with his growing erection. Anticipation flooded through her for what was to come. She lifted her head

and looked down at him. What was it about this man that heated
her up faster and with more intensity than any other man she'd
every known?

Maybe it was those damn dimples. He regarded her with half
closed lids and lopsided smile. "What's the matter, baby?"

She shook her head. "Nothing."

"Then get back down here."

Her mouth found his as he turned them so that she lay on her
back with him covering her. She wrapped her legs around him,
her fingers gripping his back, holding him closer.

"Better?" he whispered against her ear.

"There was nothing wrong with the way we were before."
Though having the weight of him on her and the feel of his lips
on her throat was driving her a little crazy. Her neck arched and
her hips undulated toward his. She couldn't seem to keep still,
especially not when he tilted away from her slightly, allowing
him to explore her breasts with his hands and his tongue. She
shivered as he drew her nipple into his mouth and sucked. Her
fingers gripped his shoulders, holding him where she wanted
him. Perspiration pebbled her skin and when she inhaled she
breathed in the mingled scents of their arousal.

It was too much. "Drew," she called.

He rose to his knees and looked down at her. Her legs were
still wrapped around his flanks, exposing herself to him. His
breath sucked in through his teeth. "Have mercy," he said.

She laughed, until he covered her with one of his hands and
his thumb delved inside her. Her back arched and her eyes
squeezed shut. But even as he stroked her, she felt him moving.
She opened her eyes partway to see him leaning toward the
nightstand to retrieve a condom. He rolled it on and thrust into
her without missing a beat. She sucked in a breath and her body
shivered from the feel of him filling her.

"Is that what you wanted?" he asked.

She nodded. "Come here," she said, wanting to hold him.

He leaned over to brace his hands on either side of her. His
mouth lowered to hers for a heated kiss, but she wanted more
than that from him. She wrapped her arms around him, hoping
to draw him down to her, but he didn't budge. As always, he

seemed determined to do things his way. Not that she was complaining, really. Perspiration coated her skin and her heart rate had trebled. His slow, deep thrusts drove her closer and closer to the edge.

But rather than giving her what she wanted, he pulled back from her, urging her legs farther up so that her feet braced against his chest. He thrust into her again, deeper this time. She bit her lip to withstand the wave of pleasure that coursed through her. Her hands fisted and her hips rocked against him, meeting his thrusts.

He lifted one of her feet to his lips and kissed the arch. "That's it, baby." His other hand wandered over her legs, stroking, kneading, making her squirm. And when that hand settled low on her belly and his thumb strummed over her she lost it. Ecstasy exploded in her, rippling outward. She called his name as tremors overtook her body. And still he moved inside her, prolonging her pleasure but taking none of his own.

When she started to quiet he withdrew from her, turned her on her side and lay down beside her spoon fashion. She was too spent to put up any protest at the moment, but she wondered what he was up to. She reached behind her to touch his thigh. "What are you doing?"

His arm closed around her waist and his lips explored her throat. "Giving you a moment to recuperate."

"Why?"

"Because I'm not finished yet."

No doubt. But why wasn't he? Again, not that she was complaining, but most men she knew would have been ready to finish even before she was ready to call it quits. He'd been nearly as bad off as she. She'd seen that in his face, felt it in his body. But he'd deliberately held back. Did he think he had to impress her with some he-man super-long-lasting power? Maybe he did. He of all people knew how uncelibate she'd been. He knew the volume, anyway, if not details. For all she knew he wondered how he measured among the others. Damn men and their egos.

Still, she wanted him again and she was tired of waiting. She rolled onto her stomach and rested her head on her arms facing him. "How long is this break supposed to last?"

He brushed her damp hair from her face. "Why?"

From the lopsided grin on his face, she knew he knew damn well why. "If I have to spell it out, I'm not going to let you do it."

Chuckling, he leaned down and kissed her shoulder. His hand on her back stirred to life, skimming lower to caress her backside. She inhaled and her breath came out on a sigh. His lips moved over her back, leaving moist kisses on her heated skin as his hand squeezed her buttocks. Restlessness claimed her, making her squirm. She called his name and he joined her then, straddling her and thrusting into her. She cried out—she couldn't help it, not that she'd tried.

He leaned down so that their bodies touched, but she bore none of his weight. "Shh, baby," he whispered against her ear. Then his lips were at her throat and his hand slid beneath her to cup one breast in his palm. He moved inside her with the same deep, deliberate strokes, but this time it felt more intense than before, maybe because he was holding her. "Oh God, Drew," she moaned.

He tilted her back so that he could slip his other hand beneath her. He pulled her tighter against him and one of his legs moved to cover her two. "I'm here, baby."

She already knew that. Smiling, she laced her fingers with his. With him behind her, in her, around her, she felt like she was burning up. But more than that, she felt protected, safe, warm and in a way that had nothing to do with the heat of their coupling. Her orgasm came with such intensity that he had to hold on to her to keep her from coming off the bed. His body shuddered a moment later as he groaned his release against her ear.

Afterward, they lay together a long time. As their bodies cooled, he leaned down to pull the covers over them. Sated, content, warm and still in Drew's arms, Zaria fell asleep.

She was still in his arms when she awoke the next morning. He lay on his side with his arm across her waist. There was no sound of snoring to tell her if he was awake or still asleep.

She smiled and let out a sleepy sigh. A girl could get used to having Andrew Grissom around, a man who didn't lack sexual inventiveness and gave her some of the most shattering orgasms of her life. To top it off, he'd practically confessed to her that he'd been falling for her.

She hadn't really believed that. She'd thought he'd confused an ordinary case of lust with something else, since they were friends long before they got to the bedroom. That's what she'd thought until that last time. There was something tender, almost worshipful about the way he'd held her, touched her. A man didn't make love to a woman like that unless he felt something for her. Damn.

She'd gone into this thinking they'd have some uncomplicated little fling that could end with their friendship still intact. Even without considering Drew's feelings she knew she was in too deep already. She hadn't held anything back, a novelty for her. Most of the men she'd dated were so full of themselves and what they'd wanted that she'd felt the need to keep herself in check. That's why none of them had lasted more than a few months. Who could live like that?

With Drew it was different. He gave her the freedom to be herself. It was a heady feeling, one she would miss when it was gone.

Drew stirred, tightening his grip on her. "Morning," he said in a groggy voice.

"Morning," she echoed.

He nuzzled her ear, tickling her. "How long have you been awake?"

"Not long." She laced her fingers with his. He spooned closer with her, rubbing his early-morning erection against her. "Were you planning to do something with that?"

"Maybe."

She looked over her shoulder to see his face. The expression in his eyes was intense. Again, she wondered what he was thinking. He'd as much as confessed that he was falling for her, shocking as that was. She hadn't really believed that until they'd spent the night together. She had no idea what she planned to do about that. If her emotions had been in turmoil before, they were scrambled now. She only knew she wanted to enjoy what they had for as long as it lasted.

She turned to face him. "Let me help you make up your mind," she said, then pressed her open mouth to his.

"What's on the agenda today?" Drew asked Zaria later, once they'd made it out of bed, showered and eaten. They were still at the table, lingering over coffee.

Zaria set her cup down. "Maybe we should give Schraft a call. Who knows if those two bothered to let him know this thing is still on?"

Drew had already called before joining her in the shower. They hadn't. "He already knows. He wants us to report in this afternoon. What else?"

Undercover officers didn't usually report into the precinct out of which they operated, at least not while the operation was still going on. Then again, they weren't UC for the NYPD, were they? She shrugged. "I can't call Acevedo. I have to wait for him to get in touch." She sighed.

"What is it, baby?"

"Believe it or not, I miss my cat."

He shook his head. "The one you claim you don't want?"

"Yeah. Who'd have thunk it?"

"If you really want to, we can go get him." They'd already blown the layer of distance Schraft's apartment provided. If Acevedo knew anything or intended to act on it, he probably would have done so already.

She slipped from her chair to plant herself on his lap and circle her arms around his neck. "Thank you."

Since he hadn't done all that much, he wondered at her show of gratitude. "For what?"

She shrugged. "I'm going to get ready to go."

Drew huffed out a breath. Why'd she have to wait until now to start keeping things from him? Since it appeared to be a good thing, he'd let it slide. But as she rose to her feet and started to walk away from him, he swatted her bottom.

She looked back at him with an expression that said she'd get him later for that. He could only hope.

Collecting the cat from Zaria's neighbor took only a few minutes. While there, Zaria grabbed some more clothes and her mail from the overstuffed box. Since she didn't have a carrier for him, Zaria kept Scratchy on her lap, stroking him as Drew drove. The cat purred loudly. Drew could understand how he felt since her hand had the same effect on him. He reached over and rubbed the cat's head. "I hope you know how to share, buddy, or you and I are going to have words."

Zaria just laughed.

Zaria hadn't asked and Drew hadn't bothered to inform her that the sarge didn't want to see them at the station house but at the Pelham Diner off Gun Hill Road, near the entrance to the southbound New England. It was after lunchtime, but neither of them had eaten. They found Schraft in the back dining room that was empty except for the one booth.

"Hey, boss," Zaria said, sliding in across from Schraft. Drew slid in beside her, crowding her, but that couldn't be helped. The booth wasn't that big.

Schraft looked from one of them to the other. "Hey, yourselves. How's the investigation going?"

She wondered if Schraft really cared or if he was making small talk. Either way, she was glad to let Drew do the talking. She opened the menu on the table in front of her and looked through it—a pretty standard array of items, but she knew the food here was good.

"Are you guys hungry?" Schraft asked after a moment. "I ordered the brisket."

The waitress came to deliver Schraft's order and take theirs. When she left, Schraft sampled his meal. Zaria watched him, wondering when he'd get down to what he really wanted. Any discussion of the case could have been handled over the phone. "How is it?"

Schraft wiped a bit of sauce from his chin. "Not bad." Then he regarded each of them. "So how's it going between you two?"

She said, "Fine."

Drew asked, "Why?"

Schraft shook his head and took a sip of his iced tea. "I figured as much. You two do realize the department has regulations about members of the same squad, um, fraternizing, shall we say?"

"How do you know we are guilty of fraternizing, as you put it?"

That came from Drew, who stared back at their superior with a deadly gaze. She could understand Drew's indignation at Schraft's comment. She felt it, too, but no good could come from him kicking their boss's behind.

Schraft seemed unfazed by Drew's animus. "For one thing, you were both staying at the apartment. That's easily explained by necessity. But since then you've both been staying at Grissom's place."

He said the last of it looking at her as if suggesting she should offer some alternate explanation. There was none, so she said nothing. But she did wonder how he knew.

"Did you think I'd let two of my people go without having some means of keeping tabs on them?"

She hadn't really considered it. For all she knew the damn apartment was wired for sound. If that were true, anyone listening had heard a hell of a lot more than they needed to.

"Look," Schraft continued. "I'm the last one to judge. These things happen. As long as it's not an issue when you get back on the job, I don't care. That's why I wanted to meet you before you get back to the house."

Schraft stood and tossed enough bills on the table to cover his unfinished meal. "Let me know when you guys are ready to go back to work." He turned on his heel and left.

Zaria watched his departure for a moment then turned to Drew. "That was fun."

He brushed her hair over her shoulder then wrapped his arm around her. "Sorry about that."

"What do you have to be sorry for? I do remember us both being in the same bed together."

"If I'd known what he wanted to talk to us about, I would have met him myself."

Zaria ground her teeth together. What was it going to take to convince this man to go back to viewing her as an equal? "Hey, he-man, your job is to protect and serve the public, not me. I can take care of myself."

He didn't say anything to that, as the waitress returned with their meal. But between what Schraft had to say and Drew's reaction to it, she'd lost her appetite. She managed to finish most of the pasta dish she'd ordered, only because she didn't want to invite Drew's questions if she didn't. But even if Drew didn't want to acknowledge it, Schraft was right. The team couldn't afford any repercussions from their involvement. She didn't know what she'd do about that, but the time would come soon enough when she would have to decide.

When they walked in the door the phone was ringing. Drew set down the litterbox by the door and went to answer it. "It's your dime."

Jackson's voice came through the line. "So it is. What time can Carly and I expect you tonight, or should we expect you?"

Damn. He'd forgotten he'd promised to have dinner with them tonight. He was about to beg off when he changed his mind. Both he and Zaria could stand a little normalcy after all they'd been through in the last few days. "What time is good?"

"Around seven." There was a pause. "Will it be just you or should we set another place?"

"What do you think?"

Another pause, in which Drew assumed Jackson was deciding how nosy to get, but he didn't doubt Jackson knew Zaria would be with him. Finally he said, "Glad to hear it."

Yeah, right. Jackson probably figured he'd find out first-hand later so there was no need to be inquisitive now. "Should I bring anything?"

"Just your sweet self." Jackson laughed and hung up.

Drew returned the phone to the cradle and turned to Zaria. He'd known she'd been watching him, but hadn't tried to question who was on the other end of the conversation. "That was Jackson. I promised to have dinner with them tonight. You don't mind, do you?"

"Not at all. Tell them I say hi."

"You can tell them yourself if you come with me."

"Is that what you want?"

He knew what she was asking him—if he wanted to make a public declaration to his family that they were together. Too bad she didn't know he already had. "I want you with me."

"All right."

Could she say that with a little less enthusiasm? After Schraft's confab this afternoon he couldn't blame her for being reticent about announcing their relationship to anyone. Damn, Schraft. He could understand the man's concern, but his interference couldn't have come at a worse time. Drew knew Zaria was only now acclimating herself to the idea that their being together might be more than some fling. Drew hoped Schraft hadn't cost him any ground he'd gained.

Chapter 23

Considering the wealth of Carly's company, she and Jackson lived in a modest house on the corner of a quiet block. Outside, the house was pink stucco with an Italian-tile roof. Inside, the house was warm, inviting. After all Jackson's years of practically living out of a box, Drew would always be grateful to Carly for providing Jackson with the one thing he truly needed—a home.

But it wasn't Carly who answered the door for them; it was Jackson. "Hey cuz," Jackson said in greeting. "Good to see you again, Zaria."

"Thanks for having me."

As they crossed the threshold, Drew asked, "Where's Carly?"

"Upstairs changing the baby."

That explained why Carly hadn't answered the door as she usually did, but not Jackson's subdued demeanor. That's what he could have expected from his cousin before he and Carly had hooked up, but not after, not unless she was mad at him. "What did you do this time?"

"Let's not get into that, just yet."

He led them into the living room to the right where a lone woman was seated. She stood as they approached, looking at him with something akin to expectation. Then she looked at Zaria and her jaw dropped a little. What the hell was that about?

Jackson introduced her to them as Kristen something. He couldn't make out the name and didn't bother to ask. To Jackson, he said, "Why don't we get the ladies something to drink?"

He strong-armed Jackson into the kitchen at the other end of the house. "What's going on here?"

"Slight miscalculation. Obviously, I didn't know you were bringing Zaria with you until I spoke to you this afternoon."

"Obviously."

"Well, you know how Carly is. Has she ever invited you to dinner without finding some single friend to foist on you?"

Not that he could recall. "Why didn't you tell her I wouldn't be coming alone?"

"I did, but what was she supposed to do, call her friend at the last moment and tell her not to come? Then the moment she got here the baby started cranking up. She never got a chance to mention the change in plans."

"Which are?"

"I invited one of the single guys from work to even out our little party. He's not here yet."

So now Zaria was in the living room sitting next to a woman who thought she was his date for the evening. Since there hadn't been any bloodcurdling screams from the living room, he assumed Zaria hadn't tried to off her yet. Then again, he didn't know if she harbored any proprietary feelings for him in that way. Would knowing another woman had been arranged for him make her jealous? He honestly didn't know.

As they'd spoken, Jackson had served two glasses of white wine for the ladies and retrieved beers for himself and Drew. Drew picked up the bottle intended for him and one of the wine-glasses. "I trust you'll straighten that out as soon as possible."

Jackson nodded, but Drew figured he'd handle it on his own. When he got back to the living room, he went directly to Zaria to offer her the glass. She was sitting in one corner of the sofa. Kristen was sitting at the other end. That left a space for him in the middle. No way was he going to sit there. Once Zaria took the glass, he settled on the arm next to her. Jackson, the coward, sat on the opposite sofa.

She looked back at him over her shoulder. Humor, not

jealousy, danced in her eyes. "What were you and your cousin doing in the kitchen?"

Feeling unaccountably testy all of a sudden, he said, "Later. What were you two talking about out here?"

"Kristen was telling me that she works in the mayor's office. Her father is a retired police lieutenant."

Drew said nothing to that. He knew how Zaria's mind worked. If she'd gotten down to what this woman's parents did for a living, she probably knew everything from the woman's shoe size to what she believed to be her purpose there that evening. So when she rose from the sofa claiming she was going to go see what was keeping Carly, he knew she'd done so to punish him, leaving him to explain that things were not as they appeared to be.

For a moment he watched Zaria head toward the staircase at the center of the house. Then he felt a hand on his sleeve. He turned back to find that in that short span of time Ms. Whoever had scooched over next to him, the expectant look returned to her face. "So, Drew," she said, "Zaria tells me you two work on a narcotics task force together."

Drew ground his teeth together. He'd get Zaria for this later.

Once she reached the upstairs landing, Zaria followed the sound of Carly's voice to the nursery. Zaria poked her head in the door to see Carly bouncing eighteen-month-old Sharlene on her lap and cooing to her. She'd always thought motherhood suited the other woman. "Is this a private party or can anybody join in?"

"Hey," Carly said, a warm smile on her face. "Get in here. I didn't know if I'd get a chance to talk with you alone tonight."

Zaria crossed the room to bend down for Carly's kiss on the cheek as Carly leaned up. She placed a kiss on the top of the baby's head. "How's it going?"

"I'm just ready to kill my husband, that's all. I told him to remind Drew about this dinner days ago."

Even if he had, the result probably would have been the same. Zaria took a seat in the only other chair in the room, a rocker. "Sorry to be the monkey throwing the wrench in your plans."

Carly waved a hand dismissively. "It's not a problem. I had

this thing catered so the food is not a problem. Besides, I couldn't be happier about the reason. You and Drew together— how did it happen?"

This was what Zaria had dreaded when Drew asked her to come with him tonight. She knew Carly would ask what was going on between her and Drew. Being that she and Jackson were his only family, she had every right to. Zaria just didn't know what to tell her.

Zaria shrugged, hoping to divert Carly from the real answer she wanted with humor. "One minute we were in a strip club, the next moment we were stripping off each other's clothes."

"You guys were in a strip club?"

Zaria held up her hand to forestall further questions. "It was work-related."

"I should hope so." Carly adjusted the baby on her lap. "Is that all it is for you, a sex thing?"

She knew better than to answer that sort of question. "Why?"

"Because it isn't for Drew, understand that. I think Jackson and I knew he was falling for you before he did."

"And yet you invited another woman here for him when you knew his feelings?"

"If I'd thought there was any chance of him getting anywhere with you, I wouldn't have. I was trying to get him to focus on some decent woman instead of his bimbette de jour collection while he waited around for you to notice him."

Okay, so Carly could give as good as she got. "Touché."

"Look, you don't have to worry about Kristen. Jackson invited some guy from work to round out the event."

If Zaria had been worried, she wouldn't have left Drew downstairs with her. And she supposed she owed it to Carly to put her at ease as best she could. "It's not just a sex thing with me. I don't know what it is. Make no mistake, I do love him. He's my best friend. But I never looked at him any other way before."

"Why not?"

She didn't have an easy answer for that, either. "I don't know."

Carly's face grew serious. "Just don't hurt him. You have no idea who would come out of the woodwork to defend him. I know sometimes he seems like he doesn't give a damn about anything, but he's been there for a lot of people, Jackson and myself included. Besides, my mother is a personal friend of your boss."

"Schraft?"

Carly grinned. "The mayor."

Jeez, that was good to know. Zaria rocked back in her chair, watching mother and baby together. But what exactly was Carly trying to threaten her with? Probably nothing. She probably just wanted to let her know how much she and others cared for Drew. It was no stretch for Zaria to believe that. But she also knew something else. Though Carly had never been anything but gracious to her, she realized Carly held her obliviousness to Drew's feelings against her. Zaria could understand that. Even though Drew implied it had been only months since his feelings had started to change, Carly implied it had been longer than that. Damn.

Again, she wondered why he hadn't told her, but she thought she knew the answer now. He knew she wouldn't take him seriously and he was protective enough of himself not to want to risk her rejection. Which meant that, despite everything he led her to believe about him, someone had hurt him before. She already knew his relationship with his mother hadn't been the greatest, but that didn't seem to bother him. To her mind, that left only his ex-wife, but he joked about that marriage as if it had been some youthful indiscretion better left unexplored. Now she didn't know what to think.

Carly stood and there was a smile on her face. "I think I've punished my husband enough. Let's go downstairs."

Zaria had the feeling Carly had enjoyed zinging her and watching her reaction that she hadn't bothered to guard. Still, she stood and followed Carly downstairs to the living room. They'd barely made it to the entranceway when the baby started to fret to be put down. Carly leaned down and set her on the floor.

Zaria assumed she wanted to get to her father, but she toddled over to Drew, who was now sitting on the sofa, and grabbed onto his leg. "Unca Do," she called.

"Hey, baby girl," Drew said, lifting her onto his lap.

For a moment Zaria leaned her shoulder against the archway wall, watching the pair. She'd seen Drew with the baby before, but she'd never really paid attention. He smiled at the little girl while she showered him with slobbery kisses, grabbed hold of his nose and committed other indignities to him. Jackson said something to him and he laughed full out, a sound she realized she hadn't heard in a very long time.

Who was this man she thought she knew everything about? As she watched him, his head turned and his gaze snagged with hers. His eyebrows knitted as if to ask, "What's wrong?"

She shook her head, turning away, as the doorbell sounded. Jackson rose from his seat to answer it. Only then did Zaria become aware that Carly was still standing beside her. From the doorway came the sound of Jackson's voice mingled with that of another man's. The mystery guest had arrived.

A moment later, Jackson came back into the room with the most beautiful man Zaria had ever seen not staring back at her from a magazine cover. Amber eyes, long lashes, chiseled features, particularly his mouth, over a body that looked lean and just as well defined. And this guy was a cop?

"You're drooling," she heard Drew say beside her.

She hadn't noticed him coming up to her, but she did snap her mouth shut. She focused on Carly, to whom Jackson was introducing the new guest. Carly's thunderstruck expression must be what her face had looked like a second ago. Zaria elbowed the other woman.

"Um, um, pleased to meet you," Carly said, shaking the newcomer's outstretched hand.

Next it was Zaria's turn as Jackson introduced the man to all assembled. Even Drew's "date" had risen from her seat, looking the most dazed of all.

As the men moved off, Carly grabbed Zaria's elbow. "Why don't you help me see about dinner in the kitchen?" When they got to the other room the two women faced each other over the counter.

Carly said, "Did you see that man my husband brought home

for dinner? Good God! I thought a man had to be airbrushed to look that good."

Zaria laughed. She'd thought the same thing herself. "At least Jackson didn't accuse you of drooling." She set her wineglass on the counter. Carly picked up the wine bottle on the counter and gestured toward her glass. Zaria nodded.

"Only because he didn't get the chance. You'd think he'd give me a heads-up that he was bringing someone like that home."

Zaria sipped from her glass as Carly got another glass and filled it halfway for herself. "Your friend out there is going to love you, anyway."

Carly sipped from her glass. "That's the thing, I hardly know her. I've already run through all my good friends a while ago. I bet she's glad I talked her into coming now. Even if he turns out to be a jerk, I wouldn't mind looking at him for a while."

"Me, neither."

"What are you two hens hatching up over here?"

Zaria turned to see Drew, who still carried the baby, coming into the kitchen. "Not a thing."

He came around to where Carly stood. "Someone's sleepy."

Carly took the baby from him and Zaria could see the little girl was sucking on her fingers and her eyes were nearly closed. "I'll be right back," Carly said. Then the bell for the back door rang. "Oh, damn, that's the caterers. Can you guys handle that? They know what to do."

Without waiting for a response, Carly moved off. Drew went to open the door. Within minutes the caterer had set up several trays with sterno burners on the counter to keep the food warm.

After they left, Drew came up behind her, wrapping his arms around her. For a moment she closed her eyes, enjoying the warmth of his big body surrounding her. His lips nuzzled the side of her throat, nibbling. "So what were you guys really up to out here?" he asked. "Drooling in private?"

She laughed. "Why? Jealous?"

He made a disgusted sound in his throat.

So, that was a no. "What's for dinner, anyway?"

His hand moved toward one of the foil-covered trays. She

smacked his hand away before it could do any damage. "Wait like everybody else."

"Aren't you hungry?"

Not particularly. Actually she was more looking forward to the time the evening ended and she could be alone with Drew.

Chapter 24

"How are you doing over there?" Drew asked as they pulled away from Jackson and Carly's place. He couldn't put his finger on it, but Zaria had been different this evening in some indefinable way. She hadn't been quiet, exactly. That would have put him on alert that something bothered her. Still she'd seemed...off somehow.

"I'm fine," came the stock answer. But she did smile at him.

Drew sighed. If he read the intent in her eyes correctly they'd be home in his bed in ten minutes and he'd never know what was on her mind. On impulse, he made a left turn, taking her to a spot he knew because it was close. By the time he cut the engine, they were surrounded by weeds on three sides.

She opened her eyes, looking around at the overgrown weeds surrounding them. "Where the hell are we?"

He chuckled. "A lifetime ago, this used to be *the* makeout spot."

"So naturally you thought of bringing me here." She gazed out the window again. "What happened to it?"

"Those damn cops kept showing up making everyone go home. Then everyone migrated to another place over on the other side of the highway."

"So is this how you misspent your youth? Luring women out to secluded places to have your way with them?"

He smiled wickedly. "Partly."

"Did you ever bring your ex-wife here?"

That surprised him, seeming to come from nowhere. Is that what she and Carly had been discussing upstairs? If they had, he couldn't imagine why. "What did Carly tell you about that?"

She shook her head. "Nothing. Ever. You've never really told me anything, either, which is what makes me curious."

"There's not much to tell." And none of it he wanted to tell her. "That was over a long, long time ago."

"Tell me anyway."

Sighing, he tilted his head back. He closed his eyes, wondering what prompted her questions. Was it idle curiosity or did something else motivate her? Either way, didn't he owe her some sort of explanation, considering how things weren't anywhere near how he'd portrayed them? Maybe not, but knowing her, she wouldn't let it drop until she got some sort of decent answer out of him. Better to get it over with than wait for her to pester it out of him.

"I saw her the first semester of my freshman year in college. We were in the same psych class. She was quiet, little, like Carly and she always looked…sad. I guess that's how I would describe it now. I probably wouldn't have noticed her at all except it was the middle of a heat wave and there she was dressed in long sleeves and turtlenecks. If I knew then what I know now, I probably would have suspected abuse of some kind. Back then I just thought she was weird.

"Next semester we end up in another class together working on the same team on a group project. The bunch of us stayed late after class and I offered her a ride home. She made me drop her down the street from where she lived. She didn't show up in class until three sessions later, after the rest of us got failing grades due to her missing part of the project. I was annoyed until I noticed the dark shading under one of her eyes. Apparently, one of the neighbors had seen her get out of some strange man's car and ratted her out to her father."

He looked down at Zaria, who looked back at him with the same unreadable expression, leaving him to wonder what she was thinking. He also knew he was stalling, taking forever to answer a question that could have been done with in a couple of sentences. And what she really wanted to know came at the end of that.

"To make a long story short, she needed to get out of her house. She'd graduated early and hadn't turned eighteen yet. One or the other of us came up with the idea of getting married as a means of getting her father to leave her alone. I don't remember which, now. It seemed like a good idea at the time."

"Then why did it end?"

"Not too long into it, she realized she wanted not just freedom from her father but freedom, period. She left, convincing some judge that she deserved half of everything I owned, including the house I had lived in my whole life. Does that answer all your questions?"

"Except one. I can understand what she saw in you, but why did you go along with it?"

"She was nice to me in a way that no woman ever had been before, except Jackson's mother before she died. For the first time, there was someone who appreciated me instead of criticizing me, someone who depended on me rather than try to bring me down. Or so I thought at the time."

Neither of them said anything for a long moment. He slid his gaze to Zaria. She offered him a sympathetic smile and touched the back of her hand to his cheek. "I'm sorry."

She had nothing to apologize for. What was past was past and he no longer felt affected by it. He caught her hand and brought her palm to his lips, then leaned over and took her waiting mouth. Her hands cradled his face and there was a softness to her kiss that was as unexpected as it was intoxicating. He felt himself drowning in it, until the cell phone in his jacket pocket rang.

Reluctantly he pulled away to answer the call. "Grissom," he barked into the phone.

"Good news," Spenser said. "It seems you found Acevedo's place right on time. We've been listening to the chatter from the place. There's some talk of a package coming in tonight."

"What do you think is in it? It could be gym equipment, for all we know. Could be drugs, could be anything."

"You and your lady still want in?"

Drew glanced over at Zaria, wondering how she'd feel if she knew Spenser had referred to her as *your* not *the*. "Yeah."

He made plans for him and Zaria to meet up with the team that was going in. They'd stay behind in one of the vehicles, but they'd be there to see what went down.

"Was that who I think it was?" Zaria asked when he hung up the phone.

"They think something is going down tonight." He told her what Spenser told him.

"Is it too soon to say yippee?"

In his estimation the answer was yes. Even if a package of some sort was delivered, they didn't know what was in it, who it was from or the answer to the big question—could they tie it to Acevedo? So far, all they had was an address on a slip of paper in his office. That wasn't conclusive proof of anything except that he knew the place existed.

But he didn't want to kill her enthusiasm. And then there was the niggling thought that if they found something tonight and they could link it to Acevedo the need for her to be with him would be over.

What would happen then? Would they go back to being work buddies and nothing more? Maybe that's what she meant by not giving it up until she had to. He couldn't imagine Zaria being willing to go back to work and pretending there was nothing between them. That kind of deception, involving people she cared about, wasn't in her nature. Since being open about it wasn't an option, that left it for one of them to transfer. He was comfortable where he was, but he'd leave in a minute if that was what it came to.

For some unknown reason, Zaria's eyes popped open in the middle of the night. Drew slumbered beside her, his arm across her waist and his nose buried against her neck. They'd fallen asleep together after a bout of lazy, erotic sex that had left her sated and exhausted. So why couldn't she sleep?

She got out of bed without waking Drew, tugged on his discarded shirt and went to the window. She looked out at the moon that had illuminated Drew's face as he'd told her about his past. What he'd told her had in some ways truly surprised her. She'd known he'd gotten married young, but not that young, and not to a woman who apparently used him as refuge from her father's cruelty.

So many things about him made sense to her now. She'd always wondered why he chose the sort of woman he did, ones who were obviously after him for what he had or what he would do for them. Maybe, if he was going to be used, he'd rather know the motives up front. It didn't surprise her anymore, either, that he'd become angry with her at the club, as he'd seen her behavior as another attempt by a woman he cared for to use him, albeit not in the same way.

Damn. What was she going to do? She'd told Carly that she'd never considered being with Drew before, but that wasn't entirely true. She'd known from the moment she'd met him that he would never play by the same rules she made other men stick to. He'd behave as he pleased, just as he did with everything else. Truth be told, she admired him for being his own man, somebody no one else could run.

As she came to know him she'd realized he was a deeper man than most people gave him credit for. She'd seen glimpses of it underneath the laid-back facade he presented. Despite the parade of women in his life, she'd always suspected that one of these days, he'd fall hard and fast for some woman and that would be that.

She'd settled for his friendship, believing that's what she truly wanted. Friendship with Drew was safe, since there was relatively little either of them could do to mess that up. She'd lost enough in this lifetime to know she didn't want to lose anything else that truly mattered to her. She hadn't realized it at the time, but even the decision to change her name had been born out of a desire to avoid pain, to make it as if all those people who had left her—her mother and father and even her other grandmother who'd died when she was nine—had never exited and laid no claim to her.

When it came down to it, she'd rather be alone, or with someone who cared for her more than she reciprocated, than to risk giving her whole heart to anyone. Instead, she gave her soul to her job that, at times, offered her disappointment, but lacked the capacity to really hurt her.

But now she'd gone and blown her safe haven, risking both her security at work and the comfort of her friendship with Drew. She was falling for him and there didn't seem to be anything she could do about that. The more she learned about him, the deeper she fell. Worse yet, she didn't know if she'd want to stop it if she could.

Hearing the rustling of covers, she looked over her shoulder to the bed. Drew was facing her, leaning up on one elbow watching her. "Couldn't sleep?"

"Something like that."

"Come here." He lifted the covers in invitation.

She tossed off his shirt and went to him, burying her nose against his neck. He pulled the blanket over her and his arms closed around her. His lips left a trail of kisses along her hairline. But he didn't question her, for which she was grateful. For the first time in a very long time, she was scared shitless in a way that had nothing to do with the job. She didn't want to have to tell him that, first of all, because he'd never done anything to inspire such fear in her, and second because, unlike him, she'd never risked enough of her heart to anyone in any way other than platonically to have a true idea of what she feared. Feeling like a coward, she burrowed closer to him.

He stroked his hand over her hair. "Go back to sleep, baby."

She pretended to drift off so he wouldn't worry about her, but it was a long time before she slept.

Drew checked his watch for the fourth time in the last hour. They'd been sitting in an unmarked van parked across the street and a little ways down from the storefront since a little after dark. It was now a little after one in the morning and still nothing. It was a good thing he wouldn't have to get out since the leg he'd injured had stiffened up on him and his head throbbed.

As far as Drew understood the setup, there were several observers up on rooftops waiting to spot whatever vehicle would pull up. Several agents in vehicles waited to rush in when the signal was given. They wouldn't move until the package was removed from the van and taken into the building. Then there could be no question as to its intended destination. Pretty standard stuff. If only said vehicle would hurry up and show up before the powers that be decided to shut it down for the night.

A voice crackled over the radio. "A white van heading north on Needham."

Since it was the first vehicle moving in the area in the last couple of hours, that put everyone on alert. Spenser said into the radio, "Everybody get ready."

Drew felt his own adrenaline rise as the van turned right onto the block and parked in front of the store. He glanced at Zaria. She had a pair of night-vision binoculars up to the window, ignoring him. So be it. Let her have her moment.

He returned his gaze to the van and the two men who got out of the front. They headed toward the back of the van, but before they could get the doors open, a third man rushed out from the inside, waving his arms. At first he looked like he was trying to shoo them away.

"What's going on?" Spenser asked.

At the same time, the tech in the van who'd been listening to the chatter disconnected the headphone wire, filling the van with sound.

"How stupid you gotta be, *pendejo*. Take it around the back."

"Gun," Zaria said.

Drew saw it then in the hand of the third man.

Gonzales said into the microphone, "Go, everybody, go."

Spenser gave Gonzales a look that could have frozen water, but he brought the van to life, pulled away from the curb to screech to a halt behind the other van. As the other units moved in, the three men started to scatter. Spenser and Gonzales got out, and for a moment there was a flurry of activity as agents in raid jackets emblazoned with the name of their agency tracked down the three men and stormed inside the storefront.

"Come on," Drew said to Zaria. They climbed into the seats Gonzales and Spenser vacated, giving them a bird's-eye view of the action and whatever was discovered in that van.

"How much do you want to bet that Spenser kicks Gonzales's ass before the night is over?"

Drew chuckled. "There's something I've always wanted to ask you. What exactly is a *pendejo,* anyway?"

"Literally, I think it's a single pubic hair, but you can put your own spin on it."

A couple of agents were working to get the doors of the van open. Not only were they locked but chained shut. They must not have rounded up the one with the keys yet and decided not to wait.

The chain was cut from the door with a pair of bolt cutters and the door pried open. What lay inside was the one possibility that no one had voiced out loud: thirteen people, mostly women, chained together to the inside of the van.

Chapter 25

"*Madre de Dios*," Zaria whispered, looking at the frightened, dirty faces of the people crowded into that van. Even with the windows closed, the stench from the other vehicle reached her. How long had they been forced to stay in there? Not only men and women, but children chained together, like human cattle. Given Acevedo's business, she could imagine what fate awaited those children had they not intervened.

She looked at Drew, feeling his hand on her arm. She knew, in part, his gesture served as a restraint, but she had no intention of getting out and possibly putting them in danger. The agents had already rounded up the three men who'd run away, plus two more from inside. Any one of them could give her and Drew away to Acevedo.

"I'm not going anywhere," she said to reassure Drew.

"Then why is your hand on the door handle?"

She hadn't realized it was. She put it in her lap. "What's going to happen to them?" It was a rhetorical question, more for herself than one for Drew to answer.

He put his hand in her lap, lacing his fingers with hers. "I don't know, baby."

She smiled up at him. "Maybe Gonzales doesn't get his ass kicked tonight after all."

"Maybe not." Drew squeezed her hand. "I don't think anyone will mind if we borrow this vehicle to get back to the van."

She shook her head. She doubted Drew gave a damn what anyone thought. Those words were meant to appease her before he did what he wanted. She didn't really care. There was nothing they could do here. She felt disgusted by what she'd seen, what one human would do to others. She'd seen some pretty awful things in her life and during her career. She hoped she never lost that gut reaction, that revulsion to depravity.

For now, she wanted to go home. She wanted to be with Drew. Then she wanted to make sure Acevedo got everything he had coming to him.

Scratchy was waiting for her when Drew opened the door. He wound around her legs until she picked him up. "What have you been up to, furball?" she asked him. Scratchy licked his lips and meowed.

Drew came up beside her and rubbed Scratchy's head. "I think he's talking to you. He says he wants his name to be Hector."

"I suppose Scratchy is a bit undignified. It was all I could think of at the time."

Drew slung his arm around her shoulders, leading her toward the stairs. "Ready for bed?"

She sighed. "More than ready."

"Then I'll be magnanimous and let you use the bathroom first." They had reached the bottom of the stairs. He nodded toward the upper landing.

"Aren't you coming?"

"In a minute."

She shrugged and headed up the stairs. He was obviously up to something, but she was too tired to even attempt to puzzle it out. She went straight to the bathroom to scrub her face, brush her teeth and dab some water on all the important places. When she exited the room wearing only one of Drew's towels, she noticed a flickering light coming from the bedroom. She hoped to God he hadn't turned on the TV.

But as she walked to the room, she picked up the scent. Drew must have found the patchouli candles she'd bought in the *botanica,* because now one burned on each of the two night-stands at the side of his bed. He was standing by the window, a glass of wine in his hand. Her gaze wandered over his body. He'd taken off his shirt and left his pants unbuttoned. The candlelight danced appealingly on his muscles.

"What's all this?" she asked, coming to stand beside him. He handed the glass to her.

"All what? A glass of wine and a couple of candles? I thought you could use a change of pace."

She sipped from her glass. The dark liquid warmed her insides, as much as this gesture did. He knew she'd been troubled by what had happened tonight and sought to soothe her. She didn't really need it, but she appreciated his thoughtfulness. She closed the distance between them, wrapped her free arm around his neck and kissed him. "Thank you."

He took the glass from her and downed half its remains. "Not bad."

"First time?"

"Carly and Jackson brought it back for me from Martha's Vineyard. Someone they know bottles this."

That was the second time she'd heard him mention the Vineyard. One of these days, she'd have to go up there and see what all the fuss was about. For the present, she wanted some more wine and she wanted him. She took the glass from him, drank the rest and set it on the nightstand beside her. "Come here," she said, tugging on his open waistband.

She sat on the bed, pulling him along so that he stood between her legs. "Let's get rid of these, shall we?" She unzipped his jeans and pushed them from his hips. He obliged her by stepping out of them and kicking them aside. He tried to push her backward on the bed, but she didn't budge. "Not yet," she told him. Grasping his shaft, she leaned forward and took him into her mouth.

Immediately his breath drew in and he stiffened. He called her name and his fingers tangled in her hair. Still holding him in her mouth, she circled the underside of her tongue over the top of him. He groaned and his fingers flexed.

A moment later, he succeeded in pushing her back on the bed. He came over her, covering her, while his hands held hers against the mattress. "I wasn't finished," she teased.

"I almost was."

She wouldn't have minded. She didn't object now as he used one hand to get a condom from the drawer and rolled it on. His other hand kept hers trapped above her head. She shivered as he eased inside her. She wrapped her legs around his flanks, loving the feel of him filling her.

He laced both of his hands with hers as they moved together. Already she could feel the tension building in her body, seeking release. She smiled, studying his face. She loved being with this man, both in his bed and out of it. Was it such a big distance to go to loving him?

"Bad news, boss."

Jaime Acevedo glanced over at the man who stood in the doorway to his office. Victor Ramirez was one of the men paid to mind the place out in Queens. He spoke in the sort of sing-songy diction characteristic to those from Mexico, a sound Acevedo detested. His stepfather had been from Ensenada, a dirty, disgusting town, or it had been the one time he'd been there, when he buried the man in the filth which he deserved.

He brought his glass to his lips and swallowed down half the *coquito,* an eggnoglike drink one of the *viejas*—old ladies—had made for him. He'd added some brandy to it, making it more potent. Until a moment ago, he'd been feeling pretty mellow, until this Ramirez showed up.

"What news?"

"The place. It got raided."

Acevedo rose to his feet. "What are you talking about? By who?"

"*La migra* and the FBI. They were all over the place. The van pulled up and all of a sudden these guys were everywhere. They got all the guys, what was in the van, everything."

Jaime squeezed his eyes shut, his grasp on the glass nearly painful. He should have known. His operation was too hot for him to have moved so quickly to replace what he'd lost. He never would have if it hadn't been for Zaria. Luckily, Ramirez was the only one who knew the trail led back to him. Those other fools the Feds had couldn't tell them anything.

"How did you get away?"

Ramirez shrugged. "I went out for some smokes. I saw it all on my way back, then I came to tell you."

Yeah. More than likely Ramirez had been at the tittie bar a couple of blocks over. Normally Jaime would have been upset, but the twist of events left Ramirez free to warn him. But he wouldn't be telling anyone else. Jaime reached into his pocket to retrieve the .22 revolver he kept there.

"Hey, boss, who's that on the TV?"

Jaime's hand stilled. He'd forgotten about what he'd been watching, the tape from Roark's club. He'd rewound it to the spot just before Zaria came back in. Jackson was sitting alone and the girls were on the way out. He looked from the screen to Ramirez. "Why?"

Ramirez stepped closer into the room until he was only a couple of feet away from the TV. "That guy busted me about four years ago for buying H."

Jaime's mind spun, assimilating that information. "He's a cop?"

"*Puerco* through and through, man."

Jaime let a small smile form at the corner of his mouth. In Spanish as well as English the word *pig* meant police. "Thank you, Victor," he said.

Ramirez nodded and started toward the door. The moment he had his back to him, Jaime pulled the revolver from his pocket and fired twice. Ramirez crumpled wordlessly to the floor.

Jaime downed the remnants in his cup, dropped the revolver onto his coffee table and took out his phone. In ten minutes the man he called stood in the doorway of his office. He stepped over the body as if it were nothing. "Yes?"

"I have something I need you to do for me." The man listened silently as Jaime laid out his plan. "Are there any problems with that?"

"None."

"Good." He nodded toward the body. "Would you mind taking the trash with you on your way out?"

Chapter 26

"Where are you going?" Zaria asked Drew the next morning. She woke to find him already dressed.

He tucked the holster for his weapon in his waistband. "I'm going to return the Mercedes and get my car."

She'd forgotten about the other vehicle. "Where is it?"

"In the garage."

Zaria sat up, wrapping her arms around her knees. "Why don't you leave it there?"

"I want to get the van off the street."

"Why?"

"We've been seen in that. Besides, I promised Jackson I would."

Zaria shook her head and blinked. Either it was too early in the morning or she was missing something. "What has Jackson got to do with it?"

"It's his van. The last remnants from his former career as a P.I."

Since he still wasn't making any sense she decided to give it up. She tossed off the covers. "Don't you want some breakfast?"

"Nah. I'll eat when I get back."

She found his shirt from last night and her jeans and tugged them both on.

"Baby, I didn't mean for you to get up. I just wanted you to know I was going."

"It's okay." She found her slippers and put them on. "Now that I'm up, I'm hungry."

He kissed her temple as they walked down the stairs with their arms around each other. "Good, then you can do me a favor and move the van in when I get the car out."

"I should have figured as much."

Once they were outside, Drew opened the door to the van for her. "I don't know why you go to so much trouble with this thing," she said. "You don't even keep it locked."

"That's wishful thinking on my part. I keep hoping someone will steal it. I'm sick of it, but Carly won't let Jackson keep it at their house. They both have cars and the neighbors complain when they park it on the street."

"I can see why." Zaria reached across the dash to where the cell phone Drew had given her still sat. "You should be glad you didn't lose this." She tucked it into her back pocket. She figured that little piece of equipment had set him back at least a few grand.

She started the engine and waited for Drew to pull out. He didn't leave until the transfer was complete and she was back inside the house. The last thing he said to her was, "I won't be long. Take care of yourself while I'm gone."

The drive to Jared and Ariel's house wasn't a long one, but they lived on some little street off in the woods that it was a pain in the neck to get to. Drew checked his rearview mirror again. The same black truck was behind him, riding his tail so close he hadn't been able to make out the numbers on the license plate. He had half a mind to pull the guy over, but he wanted to get where he was going and back to Zaria as soon as possible.

It was just a little longer, one more light, the overpass over the New England and then the side road that led to the house. Just to be on the safe side, instead of heading right after the bridge, he'd turn left. A block or so down, there was a strip mall. He'd turn in there and see if his shadow followed.

Drew sighed. Maybe he was being paranoid. When he'd first left the house he'd sworn a beige Altima had been on his tail. He'd driven around a bit to lose him, only to have the other driver veer off as if they weren't paying any attention to him. Later, he'd picked up the monstrosity behind him.

Drew stopped at the light, looking over to the left lane as the truck pulled up beside him. The driver of the car was its only occupant, a big, bald-headed white guy wearing reflective sunglasses and a black sleeveless T-shirt that exposed massive, tattooed upper arms. As Drew watched, the man turned to look at him, grinned, then raised a big Magnum and leveled it at him.

Drew peeled off, managing to slide through oncoming traffic without being hit and onto the bridge. The truck followed, took a light hit to the back end, but kept coming. He drew his own weapon seconds before the truck careened right, slamming into him, forcing him over. The sound of metal scraping against metal grated in his ears. Not only was the truck scraping the car, but the car scraped against the guardrails of the bridge. Drew knew what this guy hoped to do. On the other side of the bridge there was a gap in the guardrail large enough for a car to fit through. He hoped to force Drew down there and if necessary finish him off while injured.

He could hope that if he wanted to. Drew stomped on the brake at the same time he jerked the steering wheel to the left. That maneuver would have sent a smaller car spinning. Instead the truck veered sideways in front of Drew to crash into the cement barrier at the end of the bridge.

Drew was out of the car and at the driver's-side window in a flash. The driver's head was pillowed by the airbag. He hadn't a hair on his head for Drew to grab hold of so he settled for his ear. He drew the man's head back, confiscated his weapon, then stuck his own gun under his chin. "Who the hell are you, and who sent you?"

God help him, he already knew the answer, but he wanted to hear it from this man's mouth.

"I don't know nothing, man. You cut me off at the light."

Drew pulled the man out of the car, forced him to the ground and cuffed him. Drew wasn't going to get anything out of him, but he needed to get out of there. Obviously, Acevedo knew about him and he doubted he'd be the only target of the man's retribution.

He heard a siren in the distance. "Come on, come on," Drew urged, though he knew they couldn't hear him. He hauled the man to his feet as the local squad car pulled to a halt in front of them.

Drew flashed them his badge. "Hold him."

"On what charge?" one of the cops who got out of the car asked.

"Attempted murder of a police officer."

Drew ran back to the Mercedes. It was damaged, but it would run. He pulled out, heading the way he'd come. Now all he could do was hope that Zaria was still okay.

Chapter 27

After Drew left, Zaria wandered around the house, restless. She hadn't felt this way since the morning after she'd thrown Harry out. She'd known something in her life had to give, and she knew it now. These past few days, she'd been falling fast and rock hard for one Officer Andrew Grissom. She'd been trying to tell herself first that it was the case, then the close proximity, then the sex, but in reality, it was him, just him.

She'd have to tone down this overprotective thing he had going on, but that would probably be solved by their not working together anymore. She didn't mind being the one to move on; that's what she wanted, anyway. Though she had no idea if this thing between them would work out, she was willing to take the risk to find out.

Scratchy wound around her feet and she bent to pick him up. Now she had two males she'd thought she didn't want. She carried the cat to the sofa and sat, propping her feet up on the coffee table. Something in her back pocket was digging into her bottom. She reached behind her and felt the fake cell phone. She was about to pull it from her pocket when the doorbell rang.

"Come on, Scratchy," she said, as she headed toward the door, carrying the cat under one arm.

Before she could get to the door, it burst open and three men poured inside. Given an instant to react, she tossed the cat at the nearest one, hoping Scratchy would at least startle the men and give her a moment to move. She turned, heading for the living room where she'd left both her gun and the keys to the van still in the garage.

Behind her she heard Scratchy hiss and one man scream, but there were still two others. She'd almost reached the coffee table when someone grabbed her from behind, lifting her off her feet. She slammed her head back, butting the man in the head. He grunted and his hold eased on her enough for her to get her elbow in his solar plexus. He did release her then. She spun around and kicked him in the groin. He went down, but she didn't have the time to duck as another man backhanded her with such force it sent her spinning backward. She went down hard on her knees and elbows. She shook her head, trying to clear it, but she looked back in time to see the same man rushing toward her. She kicked out, striking the man's knee cap with her heel. He screamed and went down, clutching his leg.

She righted herself, looking for the third man as she inched toward the coffee table where her gun still lay. She noticed what must be his blood on Drew's freshly cleaned carpet. Scratchy must have gotten him good.

She never saw him, but she felt him. Something blunt and heavy struck her temple. She crumpled to the ground in degrees, trying to turn to see her attacker as she fell. She landed sideways, but she had enough of a view in the periphery of her vision to see his face: Jaime Acevedo with deep, raw gouges where his cheek should be. And then she saw nothing.

The minute Drew pulled up in front of his house he knew something was wrong. The front door was open, maybe off its hinges. He'd called Jackson as he drove back. His car was outside as were several other police vehicles. Jackson himself was standing in the doorway by the time Drew made it up the path.

"What's going on?" Drew asked, trying to move past his cousin.

Jackson held up his hands to block him. "Don't go inside. She isn't in there."

He brushed Jackson aside. The first thing he noticed was that the table in the foyer had been upended and one of the legs was missing. He stepped farther inside and knew what Jackson had hoped to spare him from seeing. A deep red splotch stained the light beige carpet.

"We don't know whose blood that is," he heard Jackson say behind him.

No, they didn't know, but he could guess. He entered the living room. The coffee table was askew. The missing table leg lay beside it. In between the two was another, larger bloodstain. The other had been speckled, like drops. This one was soaked through.

Drew lowered his head and gritted his teeth, his belly seized as the most powerful wave of fury he'd ever felt gripped him. His hands fisted at his sides and he wanted to hit something, anything, break something.

"We don't know what happened here," he heard Jackson say.

Drew lifted his head and stared at his cousin. He didn't want to be patronized or hear any platitudes. Whatever had gone down here, she must have fought them and they'd hurt her. *If* she was still alive and *if* Acevedo had her, he'd rape and kill her. In between he'd probably give her to whatever men he had with him.

"Damn it, damn it, damn it," he bellowed, having no real vent for his anger. His fist found the wall, shattering the plaster, but that didn't make him feel any better. He needed to think, not spew his temper. Logically, it didn't make sense for Acevedo to kill her. He still wouldn't have gotten what he wanted from her. He would have taken her somewhere he could take his time and not risk discovery. But where?

He felt Jackson's hand on his arm. "What do you want me to do?"

Drew shook his head. Damned if he knew, but he appreciated his cousin's being here. Drew pulled out his cell phone and called Spencer. When he answered, Drew said, "I think Acevedo's got Zaria."

"What do you mean you think?"

"I had to go out for a minute. Some clown tried to run me off the road. When I got back she was gone. There are signs of a struggle." He didn't feel the need to elaborate further.

Spenser swore. "Where do you think he'd take her?"

"Not anywhere public. Probably not anywhere we know about."

Spenser huffed. "Hold on. Let me check a list I have of known locations."

Nothing jumped out at Drew as they went down the list. Most of the places sounded either too public to hide sneaking in some captive woman. "Anything else?" While he spoke, he glanced at Jackson, who had pulled out his cell phone, probably to call his wife. The phone was a similar model to the fake one he'd given Zaria. An image flashed in his mind of her picking it up off the van's dashboard and putting it in her pocket. Could she still have it on her?

"Give me your cell phone," he said to Jackson. Jackson looked puzzled as to why Drew would need two phones but he said a quick goodbye to Carly and handed it over. Drew dialed the appropriate number and waited a moment. The first thing he heard was static. Then he heard Acevedo say, "Why don't you shut up and keep driving."

Drew didn't know whether to be happy about that or not.

Chapter 28

The first thing Zaria was aware of was that she was moving. She knew because her stomach roiled, threatening to spill over. She noticed the catalog of injuries next. The back of her head felt like someone had hit it with a baseball bat. Her cheek burned and when she touched her tongue to the side of her mouth it stung. Her arms were bound behind her, but whoever had done it must have wrenched her arm, since her shoulder hurt. She tested the bonds. She was cuffed, not tied, and tightly. There'd be no chance to work herself free.

"I see you're finally awake," she heard Acevedo say next to her.

Then it all came rushing back to her—the struggle at Drew's place. What the hell had he whacked her with?

"How long was I out?" The car hit a bump and she realized her shoulder hurt because most of her weight was resting on it. She tried to shift to get more comfortable.

Acevedo pushed her back against the cushions. "Not that long."

She finally managed to open her eyes. She peered over at him and smiled. "We don't call that cat Scratchy for nothing."

He grabbed her hair at the scalp, tugging hard. "You're not doing yourself any favors antagonizing me." He pushed her back again.

This time, she felt something digging into her backside. The damn phone. They must not have bothered to search her. She wondered if Drew remembered her putting the thing in her pocket. If he did, he could be listening now. From what he'd told her, all he had to do was call the phone number and when it picked up he'd be able to hear whatever was going on. To anyone who looked at it, it would seem to be turned off. Even she wouldn't know if someone was listening.

On the off chance someone was, she hoped to help them find her. She made a show of looking out the window. "Where are we? The Cross Island Parkway? Long Island?"

Acevedo cast her a sharp look. Maybe she ought to keep any future hints a little more subtle.

She looked out the window again. In her mind she called to Drew, *Please be listening, please be listening.* In her heart she knew her predicament was her own fault. If she'd been paying attention instead of mooning over him she might have saved herself from this nonsense. She never would have gone to the door with a cat as her only backup.

For the moment at least she was safe. She'd already debilitated the two in the front. The guy she'd kicked in the groin was driving. Kneecap was in the passenger seat beside him. If all Acevedo want to do was kill her, she'd be dead already. He had something planned for her, of that she was certain. She only hoped they didn't get to their destination too quickly.

Then she felt Acevedo's hand on her thigh.

Drew had never felt so relieved as the moment he heard Zaria's voice. They'd been sitting out in Jackson's car waiting for some clue as to where Acevedo and the others were heading. Drew's hands shook on the steering wheel he was gripping.

"Are you sure you don't want me to drive?" Jackson asked.

"No." Drew started the car and put it into gear. "You drive like my grandmother." The only time Drew had ever seen Jackson really book it was once when Carly and her mother were in trouble.

Drew screeched off, heading in the direction of the nearby New England Thruway. Acevedo was perhaps a half hour ahead of them. But he had to obey the traffic laws; Drew didn't. Jackson had come from work, which meant he had a company car with siren and light box. Drew turned both on and leaned on the accelerator.

"You're going to get me fired."

Drew knew Jackson was teasing him. "You're one of those brilliant geniuses from the detective squad. You'll figure something out." He tossed Jackson his cell phone, asking him to call both Schraft and Spenser to tell them what they were up to.

Schraft said he'd see what he could do about getting the local cops mobilized, though they both agreed they should hang back. They didn't want Acevedo to do anything stupid seeing a lot of cars around when they didn't know which one Zaria was in.

Spenser said he was already en route to Drew's house and to wait. When Jackson relayed that to him, Drew said, "Tell him to catch up."

Traffic on the highway was jammed with people still getting to work. The siren helped, but not much. Drew knew Acevedo was in similar straits since the driver kept complaining about the traffic and Acevedo kept telling him to shut up.

They had Drew's cell phone on speakerphone connected to a microcassette recorder. It had been quiet for a moment, then he heard Zaria say, "Give it a rest, Acevedo. Right now, I'd probably throw up on you, anyway. If anything, I need to lie down."

"If he touches her, I'll—" Drew stopped himself. He wasn't in a position to do anything about it at the moment. That was his own fault. Anything he said now amounted to bluster. He glanced at Jackson. "I should have been with her. I should never have let him get to her."

"If you were thinking with your brains instead of your hormones you'd realize she was sending you a message. They're on the Long Island Expressway headed down island. You know, lie, L-I-E down."

Both of them were more clever than he gave them credit for. The traffic over the Bruckner had eased after the turn-off for the Cross Bronx Expressway. They'd eaten up ground after that. They would be on the Long Island Expressway headed east in a moment. Probably twenty minutes after that they'd be where Acevedo was now.

He had Jackson call Schraft and Spenser back to tell them where they were headed. They didn't know appreciably more than they did already. Obviously the choices of where they were heading narrowed. It would help if they knew a town or at least what car they were in. According to Schraft, they had some unmarked cars out looking for vehicles they knew Acevedo owned, but so far nothing.

They listened to the driver bitch some more. Then Acevedo heard another man say, "*Callate,* we'll be in Montauk in half an hour."

Glancing over at Jackson, Drew grinned. "Bingo."

Chapter 29

Zaria craned her neck to look up at the house the driver had pulled to a halt in front of. She couldn't see a house number, but she noticed the street they were on, Pond Road. If Drew had been listening, he knew they were in Montauk. She'd have to find a way to mention the street name without drawing Acevedo's attention. Ever since she'd made the comment about needing to lie down, he'd been watching her closely. It was probably only her comment about throwing up that had kept him off her. No man with an ego wanted that.

But her time was up. She needed Drew to find her now. Heaven only knew what would happen if they got her inside that house. If Acevedo intended for her to leave it, he wouldn't have let her see where they were taking her.

The two men in the front got out to open the back doors. The one she'd kicked in the groin looked at her warily as he helped her out. He'd be on guard against the same thing this time. Once she gained her feet, she spun around and kicked him across the throat. It wasn't a perfect effort, but it did the trick. The man staggered back, crashing into the still-open car door. Zaria threw herself to the ground, wiggling her hands under her until she could bring them in front. Then she took off, screaming, "Fire!" at the top of her lungs.

She didn't expect to get far. She was still handcuffed and the men were probably faster. But maybe she might attract some-one's attention. Maybe there would be someone to report a crazy woman screaming in the street to point Drew to her location. Something.

And then she was crashing to the ground. A man she'd never seen before, one nearly as big as Drew, tackled her. He hauled her to her feet. "Don't make me hurt you," he said.

Like him landing on her hadn't done that. But it wasn't his words that convinced her to follow him, it was the gun he pressed to her side. Breathing heavily, feeling disheartened and spent, she walked back to the house.

Her burly friend took her to a room on the second floor and left her there, closing the door behind her. Zaria surveyed the room. The only light coming in was that from outside. The walls were painted a dark crimson, or that's how it appeared in that light. The furniture was dark and antique. It reminded her of a picture of a gentleman's study from some time past she'd once seen in a magazine. What kind of warped place was this?

"Drew, if you're listening, I'm on Pond Road. I don't know the number. It's a big house, white. There's a smaller house with green shutters next door. The name on the mailbox begins with a *P*." That's all she could say for sure. "Hurry."

She needed to hurry, too. She doubted Acevedo would leave her in here long by herself. She went to the desk first. Maybe she could find a paperclip or letter opener to get the damn cuffs off or defend herself. The desk wasn't locked. She managed to open every drawer. Each one was…empty.

Damn. All this finery was for show, just like everything else about Acevedo. She scanned the room, spotting a bar in the corner. There was nothing heavy on it, like a wine bottle or a decanter. There were some glasses though. She shattered one against the bar. She'd never be able to conceal a large piece with her hands in this position, but she picked up one of the large shards that had fallen and tucked it into her front pocket as best she could. She kept a larger piece, although she knew he'd never let her hang on to it.

"What are you doing over there, Zaria?"

She turned to face him, not bothering to conceal the glass in her hand. The fine crystal glinted in the afternoon sunlight. "How very enterprising of you. Put the glass down," he said as if he were merely annoyed by her behavior.

"Did you think I was just going to let you do whatever sick things you want to do to me?"

"You don't have any choice." He closed the distance between them and slapped the glass from her hand. "We can do this the hard way or the easy way. There are two men downstairs who wouldn't mind holding you down or doing anything else I asked them to."

He grabbed her upper arm and led her over to a settee that sat against one wall. While he wasn't paying attention she retrieved the shard of glass from her pocket. He pushed her down on the settee. For the first time she saw the revolver tucked into the waistband of his pants. She'd bet that revelation was deliberate, but she had one of her own.

When he sat next to her, she said, "I should warn you that everything you've said from the time you broke through Drew's door has been listened to and recorded. The police are on their way now. They heard everything except the exact address. How much time do you think they have before they get here?"

Acevedo watched her with a supercilious expression she couldn't explain. She'd been bluffing, but how was he so sure of that? "If you don't believe me, check my back pocket. What looks like a cell phone is actually a transmitter."

He reached around her, taking his time exploring her backside before pulling the fake phone from her pocket. "You think your friend Drew was listening to you on this?" He tossed it to the floor and crushed it with his heel. "Your friend hasn't been listening to anything. He had an accident this afternoon. Another case of road rage. He's not listening to anyone anymore."

"No!" she shouted at him. "I don't believe you." Everything in her rebelled at the thought that Drew was gone. Rage bubbled up inside her. Grasping the shard, she lunged at him, slicing the cheek the cat hadn't touched. His hands came up to protect his face and she grabbed the gun. She pushed away from him and stood.

Breathing heavily, she watched Acevedo sit up, his hand covering his face. She felt a certain amount of satisfaction at having marked him for life. "You're not going to be very pretty when this is over, are you?"

Chapter 30

Drew had heard the directions Zaria had given and the urgency in that final word, "Hurry." What frightened him most was the moment the transmitter went dead. Acevedo could be doing anything to Zaria in there and he wouldn't know it. For once he wouldn't mind hearing her with him, since at least he'd know if she was all right or not.

With the help of the local police, they found the house easily. A woman had called in to say she heard someone screaming in the street, an unusual occurrence in the area, especially at this time of year when most folks had already closed their houses.

Drew was grateful for any little bit of luck they had going. The hard part would be getting Zaria out of there without her getting hurt. They decided the best means was by stealth. Since circumstances were exigent they would go in now while one of the local boys saw to getting a warrant. Some would go in the front while the others covered the back. With Jackson, Spenser, Gonzales, what agents they could round up and a few of the locals, Drew figured it would be enough.

Using the foliage on the property as a shield, they made their way up to the house. The Montauk chief had made it clear that he would give the go. It was his turf, so Drew didn't complain, as long as it was equally clear that Acevedo belonged to him.

Once they were all in place, the chief gave the order. Drew stood, and in one motion kicked the door in.

* * *

Zaria stood over Acevedo, having removed her handcuffs and having cuffed both his hands around the legs of his desk. He tugged on the wood, obviously trying to free himself. She shook her head at him. "That desk is brand-new, not like the one at Drew's house. You can fiddle with that all day, and it's not going to budge."

He gave her a sour look, but said nothing since she'd ripped off part of his shirt and used it as a gag. She imagined it must be painful, considering the cuts on his face.

Zaria shrugged and turned away. She had no more time to waste on him. She needed to figure out how she was going to get out of here with a house full of men prowling the place. Especially if what Acevedo told her was true. No one would be coming for her.

Tears stung her eyes, but she brushed them back. Now wasn't the time. She went to the door and listened. She couldn't hear anything, but that didn't mean there wasn't someone outside the door standing watch. She eased the door open. Sure enough there was a man standing there. Damn.

Then there was a loud crash, the source of which she couldn't imagine. But suddenly the house erupted with noise, men shouting, a couple of gunshots. The man in her field of vision took off, leaving her a view of the lower floor. Men and women in a variety of raid jackets had stormed the place.

Tears burned her eyes again, and this time she didn't bother to push them back. If they'd found her then Drew had to be alive. She saw him then, coming up the stairs with some other officers. She pulled the door open and waited for him while the others spread out along the floor.

For a moment, they just stared at each other. Then he closed the gap between them and pulled her into his arms. He held her to him, her hand roving over his back. In a minute she intended to scold him for being the only man out there as far as she could tell who wasn't wearing a vest. But for this one instant she needed him.

But a second later, she felt him stiffen. That's when she knew Drew noticed Acevedo in the room. He let go of her and went to where Acevedo sat. "You sick son of a bitch." He reached under the desk and flipped it over as if it were made of paper, not wood. "Get up."

Zaria could tell by Drew's stance that he wasn't going to let Acevedo just get up and leave. She feared what he would do, not for Acevedo's sake, but for his.

"Get up," Drew repeated.

"Drew, leave him alone. You can't touch him. He's cuffed."

"Then give me the keys."

"No." She stepped in front of him. Whatever retribution he wanted wasn't worth his badge.

He pushed her behind him and turned back to Acevedo. He started to lift him from the floor by his clothes when the report of a large-caliber gun sounded. Drew stiffened and a patch of crimson appeared at his side. As if in slow motion, Zaria reached for the gun she'd tucked in the back of her jeans. She spun around to see the man she'd kneecapped standing in the doorway. His arm swung in her direction. She wasn't going to be in time. Another shot echoed in the room. She flinched, figuring she'd be hit. But the man facing her slumped to the floor. When he did he revealed Jackson behind him standing in the hall. Smoke curled from the barrel of his gun.

Zaria turned to Drew. He'd slumped down to his knees. But where was Acevedo? He must have scrambled away when she wasn't looking. She spun around. He was crouched by the broad bank of windows, holding the broken glass in his hand. He glanced from her to Drew then back, a defeated expression on his face. She knew what he'd intended to do then. He'd hoped to get back to Drew and use the threat of the broken glass against his neck to make them let him out of here.

What he didn't realize was he'd turned things in her favor. "Put the weapon down and lie down on the floor." Out the corner of her eye she saw Jackson had his gun trained on Acevedo, too. "See to Drew," she told him. "This one's mine."

Jackson did as she asked, but not Acevedo. Instead, he stood, brandishing the glass. What was it about these men that they couldn't let things go when they were over? "Put it down," she ordered one last time.

"Go to hell!" Acevedo shouted. He lunged forward and she

didn't hesitate. The first shot hit him in the chest. He took another step toward her, as if the first hit had meant nothing. She fired again. This time he staggered back, tripped over the upended table and fell backward. The delicate glass couldn't hold his weight. He crashed through it, screaming all the way to the ground below.

She couldn't care less what had happened to him. She ran to where Drew lay prone on the floor. Jackson had already taken off his shirt to press it against Drew's wound, but there was a lot of blood.

She looked at Jackson in a way that asked him to tell her the truth of what he thought. "It's bad," he said.

She ran to the hallway and yelled to whoever was listening. "Officer down! We need an ambulance in here." Then she ran back to Drew's side and touched her fingertips to his cheek. He felt clammy. She'd never been so scared in her whole life.

Chapter 31

Zaria paced the waiting room of the tiny hospital in a place she didn't know, nearly going out of her mind. Carly had come to join Jackson. Schraft and the rest of the team had shown up. Gonzales and Spenser and their agents as well as the local chief and some of his boys were there, too, but still she felt alone. The only man in the world who didn't make her feel that way was in surgery fighting for his life.

Carly brought her a cup of coffee fixed the way she liked it. Zaria held it for warmth but didn't drink it.

Frisk said, "He gets hit by a car and all he gets is a couple of scratches. You think a teeny tiny bullet is going to hurt him?"

She knew Frisk meant well, but she joined in the chorus of others who said in unison, "Shut up, Frisk."

That did make her smile, the idea that Drew had all these people pulling for him. She wished her grandmother were here. One more prayer couldn't hurt.

After a while, a doctor came out to tell them that Drew came through surgery fine. Tears of relief sprang to her eyes. She didn't care who saw them. She didn't care who knew how much he meant to her. She wanted him whole and alive. Nothing else mattered.

Frisk said, "See, what did I tell you?" No one told him to shut up this time.

After a while, they let her in to see Drew. The doctor told her he'd lost a lot of blood and named some incredible amount of stitches it had taken to close his wound. He wasn't entirely out of the woods yet, though he was stable for the moment.

She paused at the doorway, looking at him. His eyes were closed and for the first time since she'd known him he seemed pale, fragile. A day ago she would have sworn that nothing was capable of felling such a strong, vital man, not to this degree. "Drew," she called.

She stepped forward to stand beside the bed. He hadn't opened his eyes. She leaned down and pressed her lips to his. Pulling back, she stroked the side of his face with the back of her hand. "You can't die on me, Drew," she whispered. "Not now."

She got no response to that, either. There was a chair behind her. She pulled it closer to the bed and sank into it. She folded her arms on the edge of the bed and rested her forehead on them. She'd been determined not to let him see her cry, but with him unconscious it didn't matter. Silently she let her tears fall.

Feeling his hand on her hair, she started. She lifted her head to look at him. His eyes were still closed. She took his hand in both of hers. Even completely out of it, he still sought to protect her. What the hell did you do with a man like that?

"Zaria."

She turned toward the door, hearing Jackson's voice. "Hey," she said.

Jackson came to stand beside her. "How is he?"

"Still out."

Jackson put a hand on her shoulder. "You need to have yourself checked out, as well." She started to protest, but he held up his hand to forestall her. "I'll stay with him, but you need to go."

Zaria sighed. It wasn't any easier to argue with a determined Jackson than it was a determined Drew. "All right. But you don't leave him. I don't care what happens."

"I promise."

It didn't surprise her that there was a doctor waiting for her outside the room. He looked at her sympathetically. "Officer Fuentes, if you come with me, we can have a quick look at you."

She followed him without complaint to a small examining room in the emergency ward. He examined her face, which was only slightly bruised, and the back of her head, which was swollen now and caked with blood. The wound had already healed too much for stitches to do any good, but he cleaned the area, marveling that X-rays showed no sign of a concussion. Afterward, he offered her a pair of scrubs to replace her own soiled and bloodstained clothes. The change of outfit made her feel slightly better, as did the knowledge that she hadn't been seriously injured. That meant that there was nothing to keep her from seeing to Drew.

Carly was waiting for her when the doctor finished up. "How are you holding up?" she asked.

Zaria sighed. "I'll be better when he wakes up."

Carly offered her a weak smile. "Come on. I'll buy you some dinner. I hear the food in this place isn't too deadly."

Though she had no appetite, Zaria managed to force some soup down her throat knowing she needed sustenance. When she'd eaten her fill she sat back in her chair assessing Carly. Zaria appreciated the other woman's calm demeanor. It helped her maintain her own. "Thank you," she told her.

Not misunderstanding the reason for Zaria's gratitude, she said, "Drew's going to be fine. I'm sure of that."

Zaria wondered how Carly could be so certain, but she didn't ask her. It was enough that Drew had someone with such utter confidence pulling for him. But she'd wasted enough time. She wanted to get back to Drew.

Chapter 32

When Drew opened his eyes he knew immediately where he was. For the second time in less than two weeks he'd landed himself in the hospital. His side ached in a way that sent him seeking a more comfortable position. He shifted a little, sending pain shooting through him. Maybe he'd better stay the way he was.

But where was Zaria? He remembered the feel of the bullet ripping into his side, falling by degrees to the floor. He remembered seeing Jackson's face hovering over him, but no more. If she were unhurt, wouldn't she be here with him?

He opened his eyes and scanned the room. Then he saw her, there on the bed next to him, her cheek resting on her hands, her body curled up in almost a fetal position. He exhaled, realizing only then that he'd been holding his breath.

The clock above the door caught his attention. It read three-fifteen. That had to be in the a.m., since not a speck of sunlight filtered into the room. How long had he been out? The last time he was awake it was morning.

He focused on Zaria again. She was moving. Her eyes blinked a few times then she focused on him. She started. "Drew?"

"Hey, gorgeous," he said to tease her, wanting to wipe the concerned look from her face. But even to his own ears his voice sounded thready and weak.

She pushed off the other bed and came to him. "Don't you dare 'hey' me, Drew Grissom. You had me worried half to death."

He lifted his hand and touched her cheek. "I'm sorry, baby."

Grasping his hand, she shook her head. "It's not your fault. You just wouldn't wake up."

He smiled, running his finger along her cheek. "Why do you think that is? Having you in my bed these past few nights, I haven't been getting any sleep."

Any other time she probably would have smacked him for that, but she turned her face and kissed the back of his hand. "How are you feeling?"

"I've been banged up worse," he answered.

She shook her head. "No, you haven't."

Maybe not, but he didn't want her worrying about him. Despite that, he felt himself tiring already. He lowered his arm and winced. She leaned over him, low enough for her breasts to graze his chest. "I'm not exactly up for that right now," he teased.

A moment later she pressed something into his right hand and folded his fingers around it. She made his thumb depress it once. "This is for pain medication. Use it if you need it."

Almost immediately he felt the medicine's effects. He closed his eyes and felt her hand soft and cool on his forehead. "Go back to sleep, Drew," she said. Sleepiness pulled at him and he obeyed.

By the next afternoon, Drew's condition had improved a great deal. His color was back, and the doctors assured Zaria his wound was healing nicely. It still looked like a ragged mess to her, but what did she know? The only thing that concerned her was that he got better.

Drew had just drifted back to sleep when Jackson poked his head in the room. "Anybody home?"

She placed a silencing finger over her lips and beckoned Jackson over to the other side of the room. "He's sleeping."

"So I gathered." He set the bag he carried on the floor and came over to join her on the bed. "How's he doing otherwise?"

"Good. No signs of fever or infection so far. The bullet did a number on the inside but didn't hit anything vital. He hasn't started flirting with the nurses yet, but that's not too far off."

He nodded toward his bag. "I brought you guys some clothes and things. I hope you don't mind, but we're keeping your cat at our house until you get back."

"I don't mind at all." Poor Scratchy deserved one hell of a treat when she got him back. "How's he behaving himself?"

"Sharlie adores him, though Carly is threatening to take a meat cleaver to him. He decided to test his claws on the dining room curtains. He's not neutered, is he?"

She had no idea. She only knew she hadn't taken care of it. "Guess not." They lapsed into silence a moment, both of them watching Drew as he slept. Finally, she added, "I never did thank you for the other day. You saved my life."

He draped his arm around her shoulders. "I only wish I'd been a bit quicker."

"Unless you've got a *death* wish, I suggest you keep your hands to yourself."

That came from Drew, who apparently wasn't as asleep as he'd led her to believe.

Jackson closed his other arm around her. "What are you going to do about it from that bed, buddy?"

Laughing, Zaria pushed out of Jackson's grasp. "Both of you need to stop acting like two-year-olds." She went over to stand beside Drew's bed. His arm came around her, urging her to perch beside him on the bed. Not too possessive.

"Hey," Jackson said, a grin on his face. "I'm not the one who made a play for the other one's woman."

Leaving alone for the minute Jackson's descriptor of her as Drew's woman, she scanned Drew's face. "*You* made a play for *Carly?*"

That sounded a little more sharp than she'd meant for it to. She didn't really care if he had or not, it just surprised her. But Drew stared back at her as if she were the pot calling the kettle black. "She took me a little more seriously than I intended."

If that were true, Zaria could believe it. Carly was an earnest woman.

"Besides," Drew continued, "she wasn't your woman at the time. I'm the one who told you to go after her in the first place."

"Yeah. Did I ever thank you for that?"

"No. No, you didn't."

"Then, thanks." Jackson stood. "On that note, I'm getting out of here. You two take care of yourselves." He shook Drew's hand and kissed her cheek before departing.

When he was gone, she turned to Drew. Lines of fatigue stretched around his eyes and mouth. "As for you, your job now is to be a convalescent. So convalesce."

His hand was back on her thigh in an instant. "Don't I even get one kiss?"

There were those damn dimples again. "Maybe one. If I don't impale myself on that forest of stubble you've got growing there."

"I'll let you shave me later."

"Oh, joy." Careful to brace herself on the mattress rather than put any of her weight on him, she leaned down to press her lips to his. That's all she planned to give him, but as she started to pull away, his hand tangled in her hair, holding her in place. His mouth covered hers again for a series of sweet sipping kisses.

When she finally pulled back, she studied his face. He was looking at her with an expression she didn't understand. Still, she was tempted to tell him that she loved him. But she figured at this point he'd assume she only came to that conclusion as a result of almost losing him, and that wasn't the case. Besides, he needed to focus on getting better. Settling what lay between them would have to wait.

As she leaned down to kiss him one more time, she heard the sound of male coughing and then Schraft's not-so-amused voice. "Did we come at a bad time?"

Zaria gritted her teeth. *Pendejo.*

Chapter 33

Drew watched as Schraft and the others filed into the room. He was tired and cranky at having been interrupted and annoyed that his fellow officers had picked that moment to show up. Mostly he was ticked because their presence had given Zaria the one thing she didn't want: exposure. Still, he held on to her with his hand on her thigh until he was sure she wouldn't bolt. To paraphrase the bard, what was seen couldn't be unseen. There was no point in acting like a couple of teenagers caught necking on the living room sofa. He'd give these folks five minutes. Then he was kicking everyone out.

Schraft took the seat by the bed, while O'Malley and Bruno took positions on the other bed. Frisk was by the window. What was the kid's fascination with mini blinds? Drew had no inclination to figure it out. He turned to Schraft. "What brings you boys all the way out here again? Don't tell me you're that big on rush-hour traffic."

Schraft's eyebrows raised a little and he noted Bruno and O'Malley exchanging a look. But it was Zaria's concerned expression that got to him. Truthfully, he hadn't intended to sound so grouchy. Zaria had been right. He needed to rest. He needed the damn pain medication, but he'd be damned before he used it. But he didn't want to make her worry, either.

He shrugged, managing not to wince when pain shot through him. "Getting shot makes me testy."

"No shit," Bruno said, getting up to go stand by the window next to Frisk.

"Anyway," Schraft said, "I thought you two might be interested in what all has happened since you landed up here."

"Acevedo's dead."

Zaria said that as if it were a fact, but in reality he knew she was seeking confirmation. He wondered how she felt about his death and her part in it. He'd missed that part of the show and they hadn't spoken about it. They hadn't spoken about anything that mattered. He had plenty to say, but he wanted to be fully aware and cognizant when he said it. Settling things between them would have to wait.

"Yes," Schraft said, "but you didn't kill him. Turns out the bastard fell into his own swimming pool and drowned. Apparently he couldn't swim."

So, if he had this right, Zaria had taken down Acevedo. He'd wondered why he could remember seeing Jackson's face above him but not hers. And that swimming pool business seemed to fit. Another example of dichotomy between what the man was and what he showed others. If he rotted in hell for real, Drew could get behind that.

Zaria shrugged, as if she didn't care, but he doubted she really felt that way. "What about the people in the van?"

"They're in Immigration's hands. They'll probably be sent back to their families. I don't know."

Schraft fell silent a moment and Drew had the feeling that there was something the other man wanted to say that was not for Zaria's ears. Not that he wouldn't tell her whatever it was, anyway, but if the man wanted to talk, he'd give him the opportunity.

He looked at Zaria, then glanced at the container on his tray that he hoped was empty. "Could you get me some water?"

The narrowed-eyed look she sent him told him she wasn't fooled. Especially since she focused on Schraft a second later. "Sure."

Since there was a faucet in the room, he upped the ante. "With some ice, please." That, they didn't have.

"Fine."

After she left, Schraft looked over his shoulder at the others. "Give us a minute, boys."

After the others left, Drew turned to Schraft. "If this is about what you guys saw when you came in—"

Schraft waved his hand, dismissing the idea. "Not entirely."

Now what the hell did that mean?

Zaria did as Drew asked and went to the cafeteria for both ice and a couple of bottles of water. She doubted he had any interest in water, either in liquid or solid form. He'd wanted to get her out of the room. One of these days he was going to pull that stunt and she'd have a surprise for him. The only reason she'd gone along with it today was that Schraft seemed to want to say something to him without her presence. Obviously, he hadn't wanted the other guys around, either, since she'd just left them back in the cafeteria drinking coffee.

As she turned the corner to the corridor that led to Drew's room she stopped short, seeing a man hovering outside the doorway dressed not in the suit she was used to seeing, but a pair of jeans and a leather jacket. Although she wasn't totally surprised to see him, his being there put her on alert.

His gaze fastened on her as she walked toward him. "Listening at keyholes, Agent Gonzales? Isn't that more the Feeb's style?"

"Actually, I was looking for you. I think you know me well enough to call me Hector."

Zaria couldn't help smiling. That's what Drew wanted to name her cat. "Okay, Hector, what's happening?"

"I think we have a problem."

"What might that be?" Acevedo was dead. As far as she knew, everyone else had been rounded up. If someone had gotten away, that wasn't really her problem. In case nobody noticed, she was the one who had gotten abducted.

Gonzales glanced toward the room. Whatever he wanted to say he figured someone in there might overhear. "*Digame,*" she said, hoping he'd catch a clue and tell her in Spanish. If Drew were listening he might be able to parse some of it out; Schraft, not so much.

"*Creo que Spenser está implicado en esto, en alguna manera.*"

Zaria blinked. So Gonzales did have a clue or two up his sleeve. But he thought Spenser was caught up in this somehow? How did that even make sense? Spenser was the one on the ball; Gonzales was the screwup. Or so both she and Drew had believed until now. This she had to hear. "Continue."

"I know you guys think I messed up a few times, and I did. The agent who was killed was a friend of mine. That's why I asked to be put on this case. That may have made me a little overzealous."

Judging by the expression on Gonzales's face, she and Drew weren't the only ones guilty of fraternizing on the job. If that was the case, she could understand him going a little haywire. But what did that have to do with Spenser? "And…" she prompted.

"When we were looking for you, Officer Grissom asked Spenser to check a list of known addresses for Acevedo as possible places he might have taken you to. The place out here was on that list, but Spenser never mentioned it."

"Maybe he missed it." Incompetence didn't equal complicity.

"I don't see how. It was right there on the first page. At the time, Spenser looked at the list and tucked it in his pocket, I thought for safekeeping. Later, when I got back to my office I checked the one on my computer. It was right there."

She had to admit Gonzales had her attention now. If they'd had the address all along, they could have had local cops waiting for them at the scene. There never would have been any need for Drew to get shot. "What else?"

"How do you think Acevedo and his men knew where to find you in the first place?"

She hadn't thought of that. They hadn't exactly been careful when they'd left the apartment the first time, but neither of them had noticed anyone tailing them. Since Acevedo was dead, she hadn't worried about it too much after. But Spenser and Gonzales had been to Drew's house.

Zaria leaned her shoulder against the wall. Something about this didn't make sense. If Spenser was involved with Acevedo, why didn't he rat them out from the beginning? Or have them killed *before* they found out anything? She voiced those concerns to Gonzales.

"Maybe he wasn't working for Acevedo."

Now that made even less sense. "Then how would he know what was going on?"

"Acevedo was the receiver. Somebody had to be the sender. Spenser is originally from Texas, still has family out there. His brother has a place on the border. Between his land and land leased from the government, he's got a couple hundred acres."

Zaria thought she knew where he was going with this now. She'd read about groups like the Minutemen, who patrolled their lands on the border, turning back or capturing folks trying to get across. Some of these groups at least claimed to turn over the people they captured to the authorities, but there had been murders and other crimes committed on these people. So what if whoever captured them loaded them on the same type of trucks that moved their produce to cities like New York or L.A. and sold them like any other product? Then you'd get Acevedo's van full of people.

"Again, why didn't Spenser warn his brother once he knew we were onto the shipment? If his brother is involved in the first place."

"A few nights ago George Spenser was shot up in what was claimed to be a hunting accident. Not everybody trying to cross is unarmed. As of yesterday morning, he was still touch and go. Maybe Spenser couldn't get through to him. We had Acevedo's home, business and cell phones tapped. If he'd called himself we would have recognized his voice."

Gonzales ran his hand through his hair. "Who knows? Think of how fast this went down. We find the address one day, the next night we hear of the shipment and the following night we intercede. By this time, I was suspicious of Spenser, not of this, but that he was trying to make me look bad. We were working around the clock and I didn't let him out of my sight to take a piss." His face colored. "Sorry."

Like she hadn't heard worse. She folded her arms and let what Gonzales said percolate in her mind a little bit. She could see Gonzales believing that Spenser had it in for him, considering Spenser had helped convince both her and Drew that Gonzales didn't know what he was doing. She also remembered the night of the raid, Spenser holding back and Gonzales pushing forward. Maybe Spenser had hoped to give his buddies some kind of heads-up.

Then again, if Spenser was coming from the shipping end of the deal, his only interest might be making sure the trail couldn't lead back to him. Only after Acevedo was implicated did it behoove Spenser to help the man out on the hopes that he wouldn't turn.

"Has anybody talked yet?"

"Acevedo's people haven't said one word, even after they found out he was dead. The guys from the van don't know anything. They're two illegals living in New Jersey some guy paid to drive, offering them enough money that they ignored the cargo they were carrying. But their description of the man matches the character picked up trying to run Officer Grissom off the road. His gun was traced back to a stolen shipment to New York. He's not talking, either."

Damn. Even if all this were true, why was he telling her? And why did she get the feeling there was something odd about the way he said the other man wasn't talking? "What do your superiors have to say about this?"

"Spenser's got more time in, better connections and not a lot of nice things to say."

In other words, whatever Spenser put in his report had served to discredit Gonzales. Anything he said about Spenser now would likely look like an attempt to get back at the man. "What do you want to do about this?"

"I just want to talk to him."

And in case he was right about Spenser, he didn't want to go it alone. Smart move, but why did he think she would help him with that? Drew was her sole focus now, and getting back to the job. She was sure that's what Schraft had come to talk to them about, at least in part. If Gonzales wanted to take down Spenser, he'd have to do it without her.

"There's one more thing to consider," Gonzales continued, as if he'd read her mind. "I picked up a tail last night, someone good. I managed to pull a *Godfather* on him and lost him."

She knew he was referring to the scene in the movie when one driver had pulled an outrageous maneuver on the Queensboro Bridge to get rid of the car following them. "You think Spenser's after you?"

"Think about it. As it stands, there are only three people from our end who might be able to figure out Spenser's part in this—you, me and Officer Grissom in there. Maybe he's not a big believer in the axiom better to be judged by twelve than carried by six. I don't know." He paused, reaching into his jacket pocket. "And if you don't think he's already taken out anyone else who could implicate him…"

He handed her a picture that bore the markings of a police photograph. She assumed the man in the photograph had been the one who'd gone after Drew. He'd taken a single shot to the head.

Gonzales said, "He never even made it to the county jail. Someone in a beige Altima took the shot and got away."

No wonder he hadn't been doing any talking. And no wonder Gonzales saved this bit of information for last—that was his convincer in case she didn't believe him. Well, he got his wish. If there was a chance Spenser was out there gunning for them, she had no choice but to act.

"Do you know where he is now?"

"He said he was taking some time off to go see his brother, but I doubt that. He's got a place about an hour inland from here."

She winked at Gonzales. "Then what are we waiting for?"

Drew focused on the door as it opened and Zaria strode in. He knew that intense look on her face and knew it boded trouble. He'd noticed she'd been gone a while, but what had happened between here and the cafeteria to bring that on? Then he noticed Gonzales following her in. His face bore a similar expression. Whatever this was, it couldn't be good.

She deposited the pitcher and bottles of water on his tray. "We need to talk."

He listened while she recounted what Gonzales had obviously just told her. As she spoke the others wandered in. Drew hated to admit Spenser had fooled him, too, which pissed him off more than the idea that the man might now be trying to kill him. And he'd been right about the other car following him, not that the information gave him much satisfaction.

"What do you want to do about this?" Schraft asked when she finished.

By now she was rifling through the bag Jackson had brought that she had set on the other bed. She'd already found her gun and shield among the other items and put each where they belonged. She nodded toward Gonzales. "We're going after him."

She wasn't asking, she was telling him what she was going to do. He glanced at Schraft and saw the put-out expression he expected. "I don't remember okaying that."

"As I remember it, I'm still on loan to his people," she said, nodding toward Gonzales.

Drew could almost hear Schraft's teeth grinding. "Then take Bruno and O'Malley with you."

She pulled one last item out of the bag, a shirt, and set it on the bag on the floor. "You guys can come if you want to, but you do exactly as I tell you." She turned around to face the window, showing the rest of the room her back. In a couple of deft moves she yanked off the scrub shirt she wore and replaced it with the other. She pulled her jacket on over that.

When she turned around, she scanned the faces of the men, all of whose faces, including his own he was sure, bore a shocked expression. "What?" she said in an annoyed tone. "If I were a guy I wouldn't even have had to turn around."

Drew knew better than to say anything to that. Besides, he knew why she'd done it. She'd feared that if she'd gone into the bathroom the others might have tried to leave without her. He doubted Gonzales would, since he'd come here seeking her help, but the others probably would.

"If you were a guy, you wouldn't be rocking that rack," Frisk said.

Drew closed his eyes, hoping Frisk's blood didn't splatter too much. But she surprised him by laughing. "Obviously you haven't seen O'Malley here without a shirt."

She came to stand beside him, facing Schraft. "I want him

moved. I can't leave him here a sitting duck on the end of nowhere. Take him to Montefiore in the Bronx."

He was about to protest being referred to as a "him" who had no choice in the matter. Then she opened the drawer in the table beside the bed and pulled out his cell phone. "Who are you calling?"

She turned on the phone, punched in a number and brought the phone to her ear. "Jackson. I want him to meet you there." In a lower voice she said, "I want someone there who'd look after you as I would."

Despite the lowered voice he was sure they'd all heard her and that she'd just insulted every man in the room. He didn't really care, and at this point he wasn't about to argue with her. "Whatever you say, baby."

She gave him a disgusted look, then concentrated on her call with Jackson. When she disconnected the call she put the phone in her pocket and turned to him. "You be careful," she said. Then she did the last thing he expected. She leaned down and kissed him. Just a peck on the lips, but it was enough to make a statement.

She pulled back and glanced at the others. "Let's go."

They cleared out, leaving him alone with Schraft and Frisk, who was back to playing with the blinds. Drew gave Schraft a sympathetic look. "Looks like you've got two of us now, boss."

Schraft's only response was a grumble.

Chapter 34

"I still don't recommend moving Officer Grissom," the doctor announced to Schraft after examining his wound.

That was already evident in the fact that it had taken the man forty-five minutes to show up for the examination he'd demanded. Or rather after that time, Schraft had gone and rounded up the man himself. Drew had slept during that time, only to awaken when the doctor started poking at him.

"It's barely been twenty-four hours since he was brought in. His blood pressure is elevated—"

Yeah, sitting around waiting for some guy to come and kill you had that effect on a guy, but Drew didn't say anything since Schraft had already interrupted.

"Is he in any immediate medical danger?"

The doctor, whose name Drew had forgotten if he'd ever known it, flushed at the forcefulness in Schraft's voice. "Well, no."

"Then we're going. Do whatever you need to do to get him ready."

The doctor left, grumbling as he went. There seemed to be a lot of that going around. Drew focused on Schraft. "You know, you don't have to do this," he said, just to see what the other man's reaction would be.

Schraft ran his hand through his nonexistent hair. "Right. And when Fuentes comes after me with a machete, you going to jump in the way?"

"Nope. Especially not after that machete comment."

Schraft made a harassed sound and turned away. Drew sighed. He probably shouldn't be giving Schraft a hard time. He knew Schraft's insistence that he be moved had nothing to do with risking Zaria's ire, nor had he meant anything by the off-the-cuff comment. If Schraft held any bias in the matter it was in the efficacy of the local PD. If he'd had any faith in them, he'd have asked for their help. And since Drew was in no shape to do anything about it, he was in no shape to argue.

The door opened and a petite nurse in white scrubs and a blue sweater poked her head in. "Sergeant Schraft?"

"Yes?"

"There's a call for you at the nurses' station, an Officer Fuentes."

Drew exhaled the breath he'd been holding since the nurse asked for Schraft. If Zaria was calling she had to be all right. But had they found Spenser or not? He guessed he'd have to wait for the other man to return to find out.

To occupy himself in the meantime, he turned his attention to Frisk. He was sitting on the other bed fiddling around with a wicked-looking knife. Drew knew lots of cops, especially those undercover, carried weapons not issued by the NYPD. Some had occasion to use them in dangerous situations. But Frisk was more likely to put his own eye out, or worse, accidentally flick the damn thing in his direction. "Whatcha doing, Frisk?" he asked.

Frisk stilled. "Nothing much." He turned the blade back and forth. "I picked this up at that flea market a couple of weeks ago I told you about."

Drew had no idea what he was talking about. "Let me see."

With obvious pride that Drew was interested, Frisk walked over. He extended the handle toward Drew.

Drew took it and stuck it under the covers. "Thanks."

Frisk blinked. Drew wanted to laugh at the comical expression of surprise on the kid's face, only that would hurt too much. That look turned mutinous a second later, as if he might try to snatch it back. "I don't think you want to get it from where I put it."

Frisk started to back away, looking aggrieved, when the door opened. All Drew could make out was a white lab coat and the hint of green scrubs with Frisk in the way. A second later, Frisk crumpled to the floor, revealing the man who'd just come in— FBI Agent William Spenser.

Chapter 35

"Shit." Drew wasn't sure if he only thought the word or actually said it until he saw the smile stretch across Spenser's face.

"That about covers it," Spenser said. "It's nothing personal, Grissom. I like you." He stepped over Frisk's prone body. "But you and your girlfriend messed things up for me big-time."

Drew wasn't listening to him. The talk was meant as a distraction. Nor did he bother to try the button to summon help. Whatever Spenser planned to do would happen before anyone got to him.

One more second and Spenser would be on him. Drew tightened his grip on the knife under the blanket hoping Spenser hadn't seen him take it off Frisk before he came into the room. About the only thing he had going for him was the element of surprise, since he lacked the strength at the moment for any kind of fight.

Spenser lunged forward and then Drew saw the knife in his hand, pointed at his throat. He would only have this one chance. He brought up his left hand to block Spenser's aim. He grasped Spenser's wrist as best he could while he brought Frisk's blade upward, sinking into Spenser's belly.

The other man jerked, his face contorting with both surprise and pain. Using what strength he had left, he pushed Spenser away from him. Spenser stumbled backward, lost his footing and fell backward landing on top of Frisk.

Drew leaned back, breathing heavily. Only then did he notice two things: Schraft bursting through the door, weapon drawn, and the searing pain in his side. He touched his hand to the place where it hurt and his hand came back bloody. He'd popped his damn stitches.

Feeling suddenly light-headed, he watched Schraft's image grow wavy, then he saw nothing at all.

The next time he woke he was in the same room, but it was daylight. And Zaria was with him. She sat in the chair next to his bed, her head down, her hair a curtain covering her face. He reached out his hand and touched her shoulder. "Baby, are you okay?"

Her head snapped up. "Drew!" She rose to her feet. "How are you feeling?"

Despite whatever they must have done to him he was feeling no pain. "Doped up. How's Frisk?"

"Aside from a slight concussion, he's fine, physically, anyway. He's beating himself up for getting himself knocked out instead of protecting you."

"He'll get over it. Remind him it was his knife I used on Spenser. Is he dead?"

"Unfortunately not. He's in protective custody down the hall. Gonzales is one of the men watching him."

Drew shifted, trying to get more comfortable, but gave it up, noticing a twinge in both his side and his shoulder. He lifted his other arm to assess the damage. He felt a bandage under the thin material of the gown. "What's this?"

She caught his hand and pulled it away. "Don't. Spenser stabbed you there. Don't you remember that?"

He remembered feeling a pain there but attributed it to muscular strain while he was trying to hold Spenser off. At the time he'd been more concerned with doing unto Spenser, not with what Spenser was doing unto him.

He focused on her sweet face. Tears stood in her eyes and her lower lip quavered. He lifted his hand from her grasp and touched her cheek. "Don't cry, baby. I'm all right."

Then she looked like she wanted to smack him. "I know that. But you know that pact you have with Jackson? The one about taking better care of yourself?"

"Yeah?"

"You're going to have to make one with me, too. I nearly lost you twice in two days. Promise me you'll never scare me like that again."

She was being completely irrational. Danger went with the job. She knew that as well as he did. He didn't bother to point that out. "I promise."

She took his hand in both of hers. "Don't think I don't know how stupid what I just asked you is. But I don't want to lose you, Drew, ever. I love you."

"I love you, too, baby."

"As far as the job goes, I don't care how we work it out at work. I'll go. You've been there longer. I just don't want a hassle with the job hanging over us."

He smiled up at her. "That's what you're worried about now?"

She shrugged. "Not really, but I want you to understand that I won't allow anything coming in the way of our being together."

He'd known that from the minute she'd kissed him in front of the others. But it was irrelevant now, anyway. He asked her the question that had plagued him since he'd awakened in the hospital the first time. "What I really want to know," Drew said, "is why you left me in Jackson's hands while you took care of Acevedo."

She laughed. "You should know by now that I stink at first-aid. I was hoping he was better at it."

"Am I interrupting something?"

Zaria froze at the sound of a voice she knew, but not well. She let go of Drew's hand and turned to face their visitor. Standing just inside the doorway was David Blake, the current chief of detectives. "Not at all."

"Good." He came to stand at Drew's bedside. "I hope you recover quickly. We need you on the job."

Drew shook the hand he extended. "Thanks."

Zaria didn't realize she was holding her breath until he turned toward her and spoke. "I hear you did some terrific work out there, Officer Fuentes."

"Thank you."

"I'd like to offer you a place on the detective squad, your pick of assignment."

For a moment she simply stared at him. This was what she'd worked for for so long. She swallowed with a throat that had gone suddenly dry. But she didn't hesitate to tell him. "Special victims."

Blake made an approving nod of his head. "We'll talk more later. It seems you have a fellow officer to tend to." He looked at Drew. "I don't suppose I have to ask you if you'd be interested?"

"Nope."

Blake smiled. "Get better, both of you." Blake turned and headed out the door.

Zaria had forgotten all about her own bumps and bruises long ago. She turned to Drew, who beamed up at her.

"Congratulations," he told her. "You got what you wanted."

She studied his face, her mouth dropping open as realization hit. This time she did smack him. "You already knew."

"Schraft told me earlier today, or yesterday, whatever. That's what he wanted to talk to me about when I sent you out of the room. When he realized something was going on between us, he went to Blake and put your name in his ear. Turns out, he already knew who you were. He heard about what you did for that narc in the apartment and thought you weren't getting proper credit."

"Schraft told *you* about this instead of *me?*"

"Apparently he didn't want to risk a similar reaction to the last time he interfered."

Zaria shook her head, unable to summon any pique about how her transfer was accomplished. "So Schraft clinched it for me? I'll have to thank him after I finish kicking his ass for not taking care of you."

"Don't be too hard on him. It was your phone call that pulled him out of the room."

"Great. Now I have to kick my own ass."

Drew started to laugh, then winced. She leaned down and kissed his forehead. "Go back to sleep, Drew. I'll be here when you wake up."

He did and she was.

Three weeks later, Drew woke Zaria with a kiss to her shoulder. "Wake up, Zaria. Your big day is about to start."

Her head jerked up and she looked in the direction of the bedside clock. "What time is it?"

Scratchy, renamed Hector, hissed and jumped off the bed.

Squinting, she brushed the hair from her face. "It's only six o'clock."

He knew she hadn't planned to rise for another half hour. He ran his hand down her back. "I wanted to give you a proper send-off on your first day."

She stared at him a moment. "You mean you want sex."

He chuckled. "Well, if we're going to be blunt about it, yes."

She shook her head. "Your doctor hasn't cleared you for that yet. You're not even back at work yet. When that happens then we'll talk."

He let his hand roam lower to smack her backside. He understood and appreciated her gentle treatment of him when he first got out of the hospital. But it had been three *long* weeks. Didn't she know how much it killed him to share the same bed with her night after night and not be with her? "I'm fine."

"Yeah, well, let's keep it that way." She leaned over and kissed the fading scar at his shoulder. The wound hadn't been deep and the damage to the muscle there minimal. Focusing her attention there now was a means of reminding him of what had been.

Then he cupped her face in his palm, stroking her face with his thumb. "Zee, you remember how annoying you found my overprotectiveness?"

"That was different. That wasn't warranted."

"Neither is yours."

"I don't want to hurt you."

He grinned. "Then be gentle with me."

She shook her head again, but she was smiling this time. "What am I going to do with you, Drew Grissom?"

"Wait a couple of minutes. I'll show you." He tilted her face up and brought his mouth to hers. Her tongue met his and immediately she made a savoring sound in her throat.

So maybe she did know how hard it had been for him to stay away from her. The kiss was fierce but her hands on him were gentle, loving. He wanted to do some exploring of his own. He pressed her onto her back and looked down at her. He stroked his hand down her side and back up to cover her breast. Remembering his promise to himself to be more expressive, he said, "Have I ever told you how beautiful you are?"

Her eyes had drifted shut. She opened them now and fastened an incredulous look on him. "What did you just say?"

He swallowed. Just what he needed. "You want me to repeat it?"

"No. No, please don't," she said, laughing. "You sounded like someone was torturing you with hot pokers to make you say that."

"Thanks a lot."

She touched her fingertips to his cheek. "Sweetie, I don't need any flowery words or sweet talk. Never have, never will. It's enough the way you look at me, the things you do with me and to me. That's what counts, Drew, not what you say. Though if you want to remind me that you love me every once in a while, I wouldn't object to that."

"I love you, Zaria."

"I love you, too, you big pain. Now are you ready to finish what we started here?"

He winked at her. "For you, baby, anytime." Then he brought his mouth down to hers.

Epilogue

The Fourth of July weekend was the traditional start of the tourist season on Martha's Vineyard, so that's when Zaria asked Drew to bring her down. She was tired of hearing about exploits of people she didn't know and couldn't quite believe Drew did.

They were all gathered at Ariel's grandmother's house for a barbecue. She'd eventually met both Ariel and Jared back in New York. But there was also Ariel's cousin Jenny, and her husband, Dan; Samantha Hathaway and her husband, Adam; Sam's sister Lupe and her husband, Joe; not to mention Carly's crazy mother, Charlotte, and her husband, John; plus the the matriarch herself, Isabel Ludlow and her second husband, Charlie. So many couples, so many kids, all of them running around underfoot. Zaria couldn't tell who belonged to whom, much less try to remember any of their names.

But she loved the closeness of the group. They seemed to have been through a lot separately and together. The women welcomed her like a long-lost sister. In fact, the women had left the men outside to do God-knew-what while they retired to the sitting room to talk.

Zaria sipped from her glass. It was the same wine she and Drew had shared one night. "I hear you know who bottles this," she said.

"It's one of the many things Charlie bottles," Isabel said. "Most of the others you don't want to know about."

The women around her shared a collective look of agreement. "Tell me," Zaria said.

"There's one brew in particular he trots out every now and again," Ariel said. "Vile stuff. It's an initiation rite of sorts."

Carly said, "Jackson couldn't keep down solid food for two days afterward."

Sam said, "Adam passed right out. One minute he was talking to me and the next he was out. By the way, none of you know that."

"Jared got so drunk, he nearly fell out of my boat." That came from Ariel.

Carly fastened a sly look on her. "It's probably Drew's turn right now."

"No." How juvenile. How just like a bunch of men.

She set her wineglass on the nearest table. "I'll be right back." When she went outside the men were seated around a wrought-iron table. Most of them seemed to be fascinated with Drew. He held a glass in his hand that he seemed to be staring into.

"What's going on?" She slid onto Drew's lap, noticing the disgruntled looks of the men around her.

"Nothing much," Drew answered.

She made a point of looking down at his glass. "Oh, is that for me?" She slipped it from his fingers before he had a chance to protest and drank half its contents. It was a little bitter, but not that bad. "Do you mind if I keep this?" She slipped off his lap and headed back inside.

The other women looked at her with wide eyes and open mouths when she went back inside, sat down and sipped from the glass. "It's really not that bad," she said. "My grandmother is old-school from Puerto Rico. If you'd tasted some of her home remedies, this is light stuff."

Later, when she and Drew lay in bed together, he groaned, clutching his stomach. "Why didn't you stop me?"

She rolled onto her stomach to look down at him. "Hey, I tried. Nobody told you to accept another glass."

"You didn't have all those guys staring at you."

"And you couldn't wuss out."

"The curse of having a male ego." He stroked her hair from her face. "How come you aren't complaining?"

"I'm a woman. We're made of sterner stuff."

"Yeah, my Superwoman, in a striped bikini."

She smiled down at him. Their life in the last few months was everything she had hoped for. What more did a woman need than a man who came home every night, made her laugh, who loved her and made her proud to be his wife? And if he ran off every now and then and did something crazy, she supposed she could live with that.

He leaned up and kissed her mouth. "I love you, Zaria."

She bit her lip and grinned at him. "I know."

"Really? What makes you so sure?"

She knew he was teasing. Their love wasn't something either of them was insecure about anymore. "Remember the candles I bought at the *botanica?*"

"Yeah."

"The woman who sold them to me told me she blessed them. When I burned them I was supposed to look into the flame. Then I would see my true love. I didn't exactly look into the flame, but it was you I saw in the candlelight."

"Don't tell me you're superstitious, too. You know Charlie and Dan and Jared are convinced their wives are witches, too."

She smiled a wicked smile. "I'll let you in on a little secret," she said. "We all are." Then she brought her mouth down to his.

Essence bestselling author

DONNA HILL

TEMPTATION AND LIES

Book #3 of T.L.C.

Nia Turner's double life as business executive
and undercover operative for covert crime-fighting
organization Tender Loving Care is getting even
more complicated. Steven Long, the man she's seeing,
suspects she's stepping out on him, and Nia's caught
in a web of lies that threatens her relationship. Will
any explanation make up for not telling the truth?

*Available the first week of February 2009
wherever books are sold.*

KIMANI™
ROMANCE

www.kimanipress.com
www.myspace.com/kimanipress

It's a complicated road from friendship to love…

Favorite author

Ann Christopher

Road to Seduction

Eric and Isabella have been best friends forever—until
now. When a road trip unleashes serious sexual tension,
Izzy's afraid falling for playboy Eric is a sure path to
heartache. And Eric's scared of ruining their cherished
friendship. Friends or lovers? They're tempted to find out.

"Christopher has a gift for storytelling."
—*Romantic Times BOOKreviews*

Available the first week of February 2009
wherever books are sold.

KIMANI™
ROMANCE

www.kimanipress.com
www.myspace.com/kimanipress   KPAC1030209

REQUEST YOUR FREE BOOKS!

2 FREE NOVELS
PLUS 2 FREE GIFTS!

KIMANI™ ROMANCE

Love's ultimate destination!

YES! Please send me 2 FREE Kimani™ Romance novels and my 2 FREE gifts (gifts are worth about $10). After receiving them, if I don't wish to receive any more books, I can return the shipping statement marked "cancel." If I don't cancel, I will receive 4 brand-new novels every month and be billed just $4.69 per book in the U.S. or $5.24 per book in Canada, plus 25¢ shipping and handling per book and applicable taxes, if any*. That's a savings of over 20% off the cover price! I understand that accepting the 2 free books and gifts places me under no obligation to buy anything. I can always return a shipment and cancel at any time. Even if I never buy another book from Kimani Press, the two free books and gifts are mine to keep forever.

168 XDN EF2D   368 XDN EF3T

Name	(PLEASE PRINT)	

Address		Apt. #

City	State/Prov.	Zip/Postal Code

Signature (if under 18, a parent or guardian must sign)

Mail to **The Reader Service:**
IN U.S.A.: P.O. Box 1867, Buffalo, NY 14240-1867
IN CANADA: P.O. Box 609, Fort Erie, Ontario L2A 5X3

Not valid to current subscribers of Kimani Romance books.

Want to try two free books from another line?
Call 1-800-873-8635 or visit www.morefreebooks.com.

* Terms and prices subject to change without notice. N.Y. residents add applicable sales tax. Canadian residents will be charged applicable provincial taxes and GST. Offer not valid in Quebec. This offer is limited to one order per household. All orders subject to approval. Credit or debit balances in a customer's account(s) may be offset by any other outstanding balance owed by or to the customer. Please allow 4 to 6 weeks for delivery. Offer available while quantities last.

Your Privacy: Kimani Press is committed to protecting your privacy. Our Privacy Policy is available online at www.eHarlequin.com or upon request from the Reader Service. From time to time we make our lists of customers available to reputable third parties who may have a product or service of interest to you. If you would prefer we not share your name and address, please check here. ☐

KROM08R